Longmans'
Simplified English Series

THE INVISIBLE
MAN

LONGMANS SIMPLIFIED ENGLISH SERIES

GENERAL EDITOR: C. KINGSLEY WILLIAMS, M.A.

*also issued in a hard cased binding

THE INVISIBLE MAN

BY

H. G. WELLS

EDITED BY

T. S. GREGORY

WITH ILLUSTRATIONS

LONGMANS

LONGMANS, GREEN AND CO LTD
London and Harlow
Associated companies, branches and representatives
throughout the world

First published in this edition 1936
Second edition (reset) 1952
The text has been slightly revised and additional
questions have been incorporated
Thirty-seventh impression 1969

SBN 582 52881 X

PRINTED IN MALTA
BY ST PAUL'S PRESS LTD

LONGMANS' SIMPLIFIED ENGLISH

SERIES

This book has been specially prepared to make enjoyable reading for people to whom English is a second or a foreign language. An English writer never thinks of avoiding unusual words, so that the learner, trying to read the book in its original form, has to turn frequently to the dictionary and so loses much of the pleasure that the book ought to give.

This series is planned for such readers. There are very few words used which are outside the learner's vocabulary.[1] These few extra words are needed for the story and are explained when they first appear. Long sentences and difficult sentence patterns have been simplified. The resulting language is good and useful English, and the simplified book keeps much of the charm and flavour of the original.

At a rather more difficult level there is *The Bridge Series,* which helps the reader to cross the gap between the limited vocabulary and structures of the *Simplified English Series* and full English.

It is the aim of these two series to enable thousands of readers to enjoy without great difficulty some of the best books written in the English language, and in doing so, to equip themselves in the pleasantest possible way, to understand and appreciate any work written in English.

[1] The 2,000 root words of the *General Service List of English Words* of the *Interim Report on Vocabulary Selection.*

INTRODUCTION AND NOTE ON THE AUTHOR

H. G. WELLS (1866–1946) was the son of a small shop-keeper, and knew poverty from the inside. Having failed to settle down as a shop-worker, he became a pupil teacher in a secondary school. At 18, he won a scholarship which helped him to read science under the famous Thomas Huxley. He took his London degree in 1888 and became a teacher of science. In 1893, he left teaching for writing. As a writer he had great influence, especially among the "newly educated". His books are of three main kinds:—

(1) Stories of strange adventure (in the manner of Swift's Gulliver's Travels) in which the writer imagines himself on the moon, or in the distant future, or in the air, and looks at human life from the outside.

(2) Stories of lower middle-class life and fun and character (*Kipps* and *The History of Mr. Polly*).

(3) Books full of discussion of human ideals and social progress.

The Outline of History (1920) and the *Short History of the World* (1922) did much to make history, not merely British history, popular among English readers.

The Invisible Man (1898) belongs to the first of the three classes mentioned above. The main idea is an old one, going back to Herodotus (who lived about 450 B.C.)—and earlier still: What will a man do if he has the power of making himself invisible?

Wells had, in early life especially, complete faith in the power of science. He believed, and had the power to make others believe, that science could provide the path to a perfect world. He knew, indeed, that no man could make himself invisible. But for long he believed that science, which had already done so much for his comfort and for the welfare of mankind, could do everything; and that books could cure wrong thinking. World War II reduced him to despair.

CONTENTS

ILLUSTRATIONS

PUBLISHER'S NOTE

This edition is issued by kind permission of Mr. H. G. Wells and Messrs. William Collins, Sons & Co., Ltd.

CHAPTER 1

THE STRANGE MAN'S ARRIVAL

THE stranger came early one wintry day in February, through a biting wind and driving snow, the last snowfall of the year. He walked over the hill from Bramblehurst Railway Station, and carried a little black bag in his thickly gloved hand. He was wrapped up from head to foot, and the brim of his soft felt hat hid every inch of his face except the shiny point of his nose; the snow had piled itself against his shoulders and chest. He almost fell into the " Coach and Horses " more dead than alive, and threw his bag down. " A fire," he cried, " in the name of human kindness! A room and a fire! " He stamped and shook the snow from his overcoat in the bar,[1] and followed Mrs. Hall, the inn-keeper's wife, into her guest-room. There he arranged to take a room in the inn, and gave her two sovereigns.

Mrs. Hall lit the fire and left him there, while she went to prepare him a meal with her own hands. A guest to stop at Iping in the winter time was an unheard-of piece of luck, and she was determined to show herself worthy of her good fortune.

She put some bacon on the fire to cook, told Millie, the maid, to get the room ready for the stranger, and carried the cloth, plates, and glasses into the parlour, and began to lay the table. Although the fire was burning brightly, she was surprised to see that her visitor still wore his hat and coat, and stood with his back to her staring out of the window at the falling snow in the yard.

His gloved hands were held behind him, and he seemed to be thinking deeply. She noticed that some melted snow that still covered his shoulders dripped upon the floor.

[1] Where drink is sold.

11

"Can I take your hat and coat, sir," she said, "and dry them in the kitchen?"

"No," he said, without turning.

She was not sure she had heard him, and was about to repeat the question.

He turned his head and looked at her over his shoulder. "I would rather keep them on," he said firmly; and she noticed that he wore big blue spectacles, and had a bushy beard over his coat collar that almost hid his face.

"Very well, sir," she said. "As you like. In a little while the room will be warmer."

He made no answer, and turned his face away from her again, and Mrs. Hall, feeling that her talk was unwelcome, finished laying the table quickly, and hurried out of the room. When she returned he was still standing there like a man of stone, his collar turned up, his dripping hat-brim turned down, almost hiding his face and ears. She put down the eggs and bacon noisily, and called rather than said to him:

"Your lunch is served, sir."

"Thank you," he said, and did not move until she was closing the door. Then he turned round and walked eagerly up to the table.

Mrs. Hall filled the mustard-pot in the kitchen, and carried it into the parlour.

She knocked and entered at once. As she did so her visitor moved quickly, so that she only saw something white disappearing behind the table. He seemed to be picking something from the floor. She put down the mustard-pot on the table, and then noticed that the overcoat and hat were hanging over a chair in front of the fire.

"I suppose I may have them to dry now?" she said, in a voice that could not be refused.

"Leave the hat," said her visitor, and turning, she saw he had raised his head and was looking at her.

For a moment she stood looking at him, too surprised to speak.

He held a white cloth over the lower part of his face, so

" SHE LOOKED AT HIS BANDAGED HEAD AND DARK GLASSES AGAIN——"

that mouth and jaws were completely hidden. But it was not that which surprised Mrs. Hall. It was the fact that all the forehead above his blue glasses was covered by a white bandage, and that another covered his ears, leaving nothing of his face to be seen excepting only his pink, pointed nose. It was bright pink, and shining, just as it had been at first. He wore a dark brown coat, with a high, black collar turned up about his neck. The thick black hair stuck out below and between the bandages. This bandaged head was so unlike what she had expected that for a moment she stood staring[1] at it.

He did not remove the cloth, but remained holding it, as she saw now, with a brown-gloved hand, and staring at her with his dark glasses. "Leave the hat," he said, through the white cloth.

She began to feel less afraid. She put the hat on the chair again by the fire. "I didn't know, sir," she began, "that——" And she stopped.

"Thank you," he said shortly, looking from her to the door, and then at her again.

"I'll have them nicely dried, sir, at once," she said, and carried his clothes out of the room. She looked at his bandaged head and dark glasses again as she was going out of the door; but he held his napkin in front of his face. She was shaking a little as she closed the door behind her. "My goodness!" she whispered. She went quite softly to the kitchen, and did not even think of asking Millie what she was doing now.

The visitor sat and listened to her footsteps. He looked at the window before he removed his napkin from his face, and began his meal again. He took a mouthful, looked again at the window, took another mouthful; then rose and, taking the napkin in his hand, walked across the room and pulled down the blind. This darkened the room. He returned happier to the table and his meal.

"The poor man's had an accident, or an operation or some-

[1] Looking steadily.

thing," said Mrs. Hall. "What a fright those bandages did give me."

She put on some more coal, and hung the traveller's coat to dry. "And the glasses! Why, he doesn't look human at all. And holding that napkin over his mouth all the time. Talking through it! . . . Perhaps his mouth was hurt too."

She turned round, as one who suddenly remembers. "Bless my soul alive!" she said, "haven't you done those potatoes *yet*, Millie?"

When Mrs. Hall went to clear away the stranger's lunch, her idea that his mouth must also have been damaged in an accident was strengthened, for though he was smoking a pipe, all the time that she was in the room he kept the lower part of his face covered. He sat in the corner with his back to the window blind, and spoke now, having eaten and drunk and being comfortably warmed through, less impatiently than before. The reflection of the fire shone red in his glasses.

"I have some boxes," he said, "at Bramblehurst Station. How can they be brought here?"

Mrs. Hall answered his question, and then, "It's a steep road by the hill, sir," she said. "It was there a carriage was upset, a year ago and more. A gentleman was killed. Accidents, sir, happen in a moment, don't they?"

"They do."

"But people take long enough to get well, sir, don't they? There was my sister's son, Tom, just cut his arm with a scythe[1] —he fell on it in the hayfield—and bless me! he was three months tied up, sir. You'd hardly believe it. I've been afraid of scythes ever since, sir."

"I can quite understand that," said the visitor.

"We were afraid that he'd have to have an operation, he was so bad, sir."

The visitor laughed suddenly—a laugh like the bark of a dog.

"*Was* he?"

"He was, sir. And no laughing matter to those who had

[1] Long, curved blade for cutting grass.

to nurse him as I had, my sister being busy with her little ones so much. There was bandages to do, sir, and bandages to undo. So that if I may be so bold as to say it, sir——"

"Will you get me some matches?" said the visitor quite suddenly. "My pipe is out."

Mrs. Hall stopped. It was certainly rude of him after telling him all she had done. But she remembered the two sovereigns . . . and went for the matches.

"Thanks," he said shortly, as she put them down, and turned his back upon her and looked out of the window again. Evidently he did not like talking about bandages.

The visitor remained in the room until four o'clock, without giving Mrs. Hall an excuse for a visit. He was very quiet during that time: perhaps he sat in the growing darkness smoking by the firelight—perhaps he slept.

Once or twice a listener might have heard him: for five minutes he could be heard walking up and down the room. He seemed to be talking to himself. Then the arm-chair creaked[1] as he sat down again.

[1] Made a sound.

CHAPTER 2

MR. TEDDY HENFREY'S FIRST IMPRESSIONS

AT four o'clock, when it was fairly dark, and Mrs. Hall was trying to find courage to go in and ask her visitor if he would take some tea, Teddy Henfrey, the clock-mender, came into the bar.

"My word, Mrs. Hall," said he, "but this is terrible snowy weather for thin boots!"

Mrs. Hall agreed, and then noticed he had his bag with him. "Now you're here, Mr. Teddy," said she, "I'd be glad if you'd look at the old clock. It is going, and it strikes loud and clear, but the hour hand does nothing but point at six."

And leading the way, she went across to the parlour door and knocked.

As she opened the door, she saw her visitor seated in the arm-chair before the fire, asleep, it seemed, with his bandaged head leaning on one side. The only light in the room was the red glow from the fire. Everything seemed hidden in shadows. But for a second it seemed to her that the man she looked at had a huge mouth wide open, a mouth that swallowed the whole of the lower part of his face. It was too ugly to believe, the white head, the staring glasses—and then a great hole. He moved, started up in his chair and put up his hand. She opened the door wide, so that the room was lighter, and she saw him more clearly, with the cloth held to his face, just as she had seen him hold it before. The shadows, she fancied, had tricked her.

"Would you mind, sir, if this man came to look at the clock, sir?" she said.

"Look at the clock?" he said, staring round sleepily and

17

speaking over his hand; and then, more fully awake, "Certainly."

Mrs. Hall went away to get a lamp, and he rose and stretched himself. Then came the light, and at the door Mr. Teddy Henfrey was met by this bandaged person. He was, he said, "quite startled."

"Good afternoon," said the stranger, staring at him—as Mr. Henfrey says—"like a fish."

"I hope," said Mr. Henfrey, "that you don't mind."

"Not at all," said the stranger. "Though I understand," he said, turning to Mrs. Hall, "that this room is really to be mine for my own use."

"I thought, sir," said Mrs. Hall, "you'd like the clock——"

"Certainly," said the stranger, "certainly; but at other times I like to be alone."

He turned round with his back to the fireplace, and put his hands behind his back. "And presently," he said, "when the clock is mended I think I should like to have some tea. But not till then."

Mrs. Hall was about to leave the room—she did not try to talk this time—when her visitor asked her if she had done anything about his boxes at Bramblehurst. She told him that the carrier could bring them over the next day.

"You are certain that is the earliest?" he said. She was quite sure.

"I should explain," he added, "what I was really too cold and tired to do before, that I am a scientist."

"Indeed, sir," said Mrs. Hall respectfully.

"And I need things from the boxes for my work."

"Of course, sir."

"My reason for coming to Iping," he went on slowly, "was . . . a desire to be alone. I do not wish to be disturbed in my work. Besides my work, an accident——"

"I thought so," said Mrs. Hall to herself.

"—makes it necessary for me to be quiet. My eyes are sometimes so weak and painful that I have to shut myself up in the dark for hours together and lock myself in. Sometimes—

now and then. Not at present, certainly. At such times the least thing, even a stranger coming into the room, gives me great pain. . . . It is well these things should be understood."

"Certainly, sir," said Mrs. Hall. "And if I might be so bold as to ask——"

"That, I think, is all," said the stranger quietly.

Mrs. Hall said no more.

After Mrs. Hall had left the room he remained standing in front of the fire, looking at the clock being mended. Mr. Henfrey worked with the lamp close to him, and the green shade threw a bright light upon his hands and upon the frame and wheels, and left the rest of the room in shadow. He took longer than he needed to remove the works, hoping to have some talk with the stranger. But the stranger stood there, perfectly silent and still. So still that it made Henfrey afraid. He felt alone in the room and looked up, and there, grey and shadowy, was the bandaged head and huge, dark glasses staring straight in front of them. It was so strange to Henfrey that for a minute they stood staring at each other. Then Henfrey looked down again. He would have liked to say something. Should he say that the weather was very cold for the time of the year?

"The weather——" he began.

"Why don't you finish and go?" said the stiff figure angrily. "All you've got to do is to fix the hour hand. You're simply wasting time."

"Certainly, sir—one minute more. I forgot. . . ." And Mr. Henfrey finished and went.

But he went off in anger. "Damn it!" said Mr. Henfrey to himself, walking down the village street through the falling snow, "a man must mend a clock sometimes, surely."

And again, "Can't a man look at you? Ugly!"

And yet again, "It seems he can't. If the police were wanting you, you couldn't be more wrapped and bandaged."

At the street corner he saw Hall, who had lately married the lady of the inn. "How do, Teddy?" said Hall, as he passed.

"You've got a strange visitor!" said Teddy.

Hall stopped. "What's that?" he asked.

"Queer man stopping at the inn," said Teddy.

And he described Mrs. Hall's guest. "Looks a bit funny, doesn't it? I'd like to see a man's face if I had him stopping in *my* house," said Henfrey. "But women are so simple with strangers. He's taken your rooms, and he hasn't even given a name."

"You don't say so," said Hall, a rather stupid man.

"Yes," said Teddy. "And he's got a lot of boxes coming to-morrow, so he says."

Teddy walked on, easier in his mind.

And after the stranger had gone to bed, which he did about half-past nine, Mr. Hall went into the parlour, and looked very hard at the furniture, just to show that the stranger wasn't master there. When he went to bed, he told Mrs. Hall to look very closely at the stranger's boxes when they came next day.

"You mind your own business, Hall," said Mrs. Hall, "and I'll mind mine."

But in the middle of the night she woke up dreaming of huge white heads that came after her, at the end of long necks, and with big black eyes. But being a sensible woman, she turned over and went to sleep again.

CHAPTER 3

THE THOUSAND AND ONE BOTTLES

THAT was how, on the 9th day of February, at the beginning of warmer weather, the stranger came to Iping village. Next day his boxes arrived. There were two trunks, indeed, such as any man might have, but also there was a box of books—big, fat books, of which some were in hand-writing you couldn't read —and a dozen or more boxes and cases full of glass bottles, as it seemed to Hall, as he pulled at the straw. The stranger, covered up in hat, coat, gloves, and overcoat, came out impatiently to meet Fearenside's cart, while Hall was having a talk with the carrier before helping to bring the boxes in. Out he came, not noticing Fearenside's dog, who was smelling at Hall's legs.

"Come along with those boxes," he said. "I've been waiting long enough."

And he came down the steps towards the back of the cart, as if to lay hands on the smaller case.

As soon as Fearenside's dog caught sight of him, however, it began to growl, and when he ran down the steps it sprang straight at his hand. Hall cried out and jumped back, for he was not very brave with dogs, and Fearenside shouted, "Lie down!" and caught up his whip.

They saw the dog's teeth had missed his hand, heard a kick, saw the dog jump and bite the stranger's leg, and heard the sound of his trousers tearing. Then Fearenside's whip reached his dog, which, howling with pain, crept under the wheels of the wagon. It was all done in a swift half minute. No one spoke, everyone shouted. The stranger looked at his torn glove and at his leg, then turned and ran up the steps into the

21

inn. They heard him go across the passage and up the stairs to his bedroom.

"You brute, you!" said Fearenside, climbing off the wagon with his whip in his hand, while the dog watched him through the wheel.

"Come here!" said Fearenside. . . . "You'd better."

Hall had stood gaping. "He was bitten," said Hall. "I'd better go and see him." And he trotted after the stranger. He met Mrs. Hall in the passage. "Carrier's dog," he said, "bit him."

He went straight upstairs, pushed open the stranger's door and went in.

The blind was down and the room dim. He caught sight of a strange thing, a handless arm that seemed to be waving towards him, and a face of three large dark spots on white. Then he was struck in the chest, thrown out of the room, and the door shut in his face, and locked. It happened so swiftly that it gave him no time to see anything clearly. A waving of shapes, a blow and a noise like a gun. There he stood in the dark little passage wondering what he had seen.

After a few minutes he came back to the little group that had formed outside the inn. There was Fearenside telling the story all over again for the second time; there was Mrs. Hall saying his dog had no right to bite her guests; there was Huxter, the shopkeeper from over the road, asking questions: and Sandy Wadgers looking solemn; besides women and children, all talking.

Mr. Hall, staring at them from the steps and listening, could not believe that he had seen anything very strange happen upstairs.

"He wants no help, he says," he said in answer to his wife's question. "We'd better take his luggage in."

"He ought to have his leg looked after at once," said Mr. Huxter.

"I'd shoot the dog, that's what I'd do," said a lady in the group.

Suddenly the dog began growling again.

"Come along," cried an angry voice in the doorway, and there stood the stranger, with his coat collar turned up and his hat brim bent down.

"The sooner you get those things in, the better I'll be pleased." His trousers and gloves had been changed.

"Were you hurt, sir?" said Fearenside. "I'm very sorry the dog——"

"Not at all," said the stranger. "It never broke the skin. Hurry up with those things."

As soon as the first box was carried into the parlour, the stranger began to unpack it, eagerly scattering the straw, and from it he brought out bottles—little fat bottles, small, thin bottles, blue bottles, bottles with round bodies and thin necks, large green glass bottles, large white glass bottles, wine bottles, bottles, bottles, bottles—putting them in rows on the table under the window, round the floor, on the shelf—everywhere. Case after case was full of bottles; he emptied six of the cases and piled the straw high on the floor and table.

And as soon as the cases were empty, the stranger went to the window and set to work, not troubling in the least about the straw, the fire which had gone out, the box of books outside, or the trunks and other things that had gone upstairs.

When Mrs. Hall took his dinner in to him, he did not hear her until she had swept away most of the straw and had put the food on the table. Then he half turned his head, and turned it away again. But she saw he had taken off his glasses; they were beside him on the table, and he seemed to her to have no eyes. He put on his glasses again, and then turned and faced her. She was about to complain of the straw on the floor, but he spoke first.

"I wish you wouldn't come in without knocking," he said, angrily as usual.

"I knocked, but——"

"But in my work I cannot have any—I must ask you——"

"Certainly, sir. You can turn the key if you want to, you know. Any time."

"A very good idea," said the stranger.

" This straw, sir. If I might say——"

" Don't. If the straw makes trouble, put it down in the bill."

He was so strange, standing there, with his bottles and his bad temper, that Mrs. Hall was quite afraid. But she was a strong-minded woman. " Then I should like to know, sir, what you consider——"

" A shilling—put down a shilling in my bill. Surely a shilling's enough? "

" Very well," said Mrs. Hall, taking up the table-cloth and beginning to spread it over the table.

" If you're satisfied, of course——"

He turned his back on her and sat down.

All the afternoon he worked with the door locked, and almost in silence. But once there was a noise of bottles ringing together, as though the table had been hit, and the smash of glass thrown down, and then came the sound of quick walking up and down the room. Fearing something was the matter, she went to the door and listened, not caring to knock.

" I can't go on," he was shouting; " I *can't* go on! Three hundred thousand, four hundred thousand! All my life it may take me! . . . Patience! Patience, indeed! . . . Fool! fool! "

There was a noise of boots on the brick floor of the bar, and Mrs. Hall could not stay to hear any more. When she returned, the room was silent again, save for the faint sound of his chair, and now and then of a bottle. It was all over; the stranger had returned to his work.

Later, when she took in his tea she saw broken glass in the corner of the room. She pointed at it.

" Put it down in the bill," he said. " For God's sake don't worry me! If there's damage done, put it down in the bill," and he went on with his writing.

" I'll tell you something," said Fearenside. It was late in the afternoon, and they were in the little inn of Iping Hanger.

" Well? " said Teddy Henfrey.

"This man you're speaking of, that my dog bit. Well—he's black. At least his legs are. I saw through the tear in his trousers and the tear in his glove. You'd have expected a sort of pink to show, wouldn't you? Well—there was just blackness. I tell you he's as black as my hat."

"Good heavens!" said Henfrey. "It's a queer case altogether. Why, his nose is as pink as paint!"

"That's true," said Fearenside. "I know that. And I tell you what I'm thinking. That man's black here and white there —in pieces. And he daren't show it. He's a kind of half-breed. I've heard of such things before. And it's common with horses, as anyone can see."

CHAPTER 4

MR. CUSS TALKS WITH THE STRANGER

THE stranger rarely went out by day, but in the evening he would go out, wrapped up to the eyes, whether the weather was cold or not, and he chose the loneliest paths. His spectacles and bandaged face under his great black hat came suddenly out of the darkness upon one or two workmen coming home, and Teddy Henfrey, coming out of the " Scarlet Coat "[1] one night at half-past nine, was frightened by the stranger's white, round head (he was walking hat in hand) lit by the sudden light of the open inn door. It seemed doubtful whether he hated boys more than they hated him, but there was certainly hatred enough on either side.

Of course they talked about him in Iping, and were unable to decide what his business was. Mrs. Hall said he " discovered things," that he had had an accident, and that he did not like people to see the ugly scars.[2] Some said that he was a criminal hiding from the police, and others that he was part white and part black, and " if he chose to show himself at fairs[3] he would make a great deal of money." A few thought that he was simply and harmlessly mad. And at last some of the women began to think that he was a ghost or a magician.

No one liked him, for he was always angry and never friendly. They drew aside as he passed down the village street, and when he had gone by, young men would put their coat collars up and pull their hat brims down, and follow him for a joke.

Cuss, the doctor, was interested in the bandages and in the bottles. All through April and May he wanted to talk to the stranger, and at last, towards Whitsuntide, he could bear it

[1] Another inn.   [2] Marks made by a wound.
[3] Where people buy and sell and amuse themselves.

26

no longer and went to visit him. He was surprised to find that Mr. Hall did not know his guest's name.

"He gave a name," said Mrs. Hall—this was untrue—"but I didn't hear it properly." She thought it seemed so silly not to know the man's name.

Cuss could hear cursing inside the parlour. He knocked at the door and entered.

"Please forgive me for breaking in upon you," said Cuss, and then the door closed and shut out Mrs. Hall.

She could hear the sound of voices for the next ten minutes, then a cry of surprise, a stirring of feet, a chair thrown aside, a laugh, quick steps to the door, and Cuss appeared, his face white, his eyes staring over his shoulder. He left the door open behind him, and, without looking at her, went across the hall and down the steps, and she heard his feet hurrying along the road. He carried his hat in his hand. She stood behind the bar, looking at the open door of the parlour. Then she heard the stranger laughing quietly, and his footsteps came across the room. She could not see his face from where she stood. The parlour door shut loudly, and the place was silent again.

Cuss went straight up the village to Bunting, the vicar.

"Am I mad?" Cuss began, as he entered the little study. "Do I look like a madman?"

"What's happened?" asked the vicar.

"That man at the inn——"

"Well?"

"Give me something to drink," said Cuss and he sat down.

When his nerves had been steadied by a glass of wine, "I went in," he said. "He'd put his hands in his pockets as I came in, and he sat down in his chair. I told him I'd heard he took an interest in scientific things. He said, 'Yes.' I tried to talk to him. He got quite angry. . . . Well, he told me that he had had a piece of paper. It was important, most important, most valuable. A list of . . . 'Was it medicine?' I asked. 'Why do you want to know?' was his answer. At any rate this paper was of great value. He had read it, put it down on the table and looked away. Then the wind had lifted it and blown it into the fire. He saw it go up the chimney. Just as he told me that, he lifted his arm. The sleeve was empty. I could see right up it. What can keep a sleeve up and open if there's nothing in it?

" ' How can you move an empty sleeve like that? ' I asked.

" ' Empty sleeve? '

" ' Yes,' I said, ' an empty sleeve.'

" ' It's an empty sleeve, is it? You saw it was an empty sleeve? ' He stood up. I stood up too. He came towards me in three very slow steps, and stood quite close.

" ' You said it was an empty sleeve? ' he said. ' Certainly,' I said. Then very quietly he pulled his sleeve out of his pocket again, and raised his arm towards me, as though he would show it to me again. He did it very, very slowly. I looked at it. Seemed an age. ' Well? ' said I, clearing my throat; ' there's nothing in it.'

" I was beginning to feel frightened. I could see right down it. He put it out straight towards me, slowly, slowly—just like that—until it was six inches from my face. Queer thing to see an empty sleeve come at you like that! And then——"

" Well? "

" Something—it felt exactly like a finger and a thumb—pulled my nose."

Bunting began to laugh.

" There wasn't anything there! " said Cuss—his voice running up into a shriek at the " there."

" You may laugh if you like, but I tell you I was so startled, I hit his sleeve hard, and turned round and ran out of the room—I left him——"

Cuss stopped. It was easy to see that he was afraid. He turned round in a helpless way, and took a second glass of wine. "When I hit his sleeve," said Cuss, "I tell you, it felt exactly like hitting an arm. And there wasn't an arm! There wasn't any arm at all! "

Mr. Bunting thought it over. "It's a very strange story," he said. He looked very wise and solemn indeed.

"It's really," said Mr. Bunting, "a very strange story."

CHAPTER 5

THE ROBBERY AT THE VICARAGE

THE robbery at the Vicarage occurred in the early hours of Whit Monday, a day devoted in Iping to festivities. Mrs. Bunting, it seems, woke up suddenly in the stillness that comes before the sunrise, with a strong feeling that the door of their bedroom had opened and closed. She did not wake her husband at first, but sat up in bed listening. She then distinctly heard the sound of bare feet coming out of the next room and walking along the passage towards the stairs. As soon as she felt sure of this, she woke the Rev. Mr. Bunting as quietly as she could. He did not light the lamp, but put on his spectacles and his bath slippers, and went out of the bedroom to listen. He heard quite clearly someone moving in his study downstairs, and then a violent sneeze.

At that he returned to his bedroom, armed himself with the poker,[1] and went downstairs as silently as he could. Mrs. Bunting stood at the top of the stairs.

It was about four o'clock, and the last darkness of the night was passed. There was a faint light in the passage; the study door stood half open. Everything was still, except the faint sound of the stairs under Mr. Bunting's tread, and the slight movements in the study. He heard a drawer being opened, and there was a rustle[2] of papers. Then came a curse, and a match was struck, and the study was full of yellow light. Mr. Bunting was now in the hall, and through the half-open door he could see the desk, an open drawer, and a candle burning on the desk. But the thief he could not see. He

[1] An iron rod for stirring the fire.
[2] A sound made when papers or dead leaves are moved together.

stood there in the hall undecided what to do, and Mrs. Bunting, her face white and set, crept slowly downstairs after him.

They heard the noise of coins, and knew that the thief had found the housekeeping money—two pounds ten shillings in half sovereigns. That sound made Mr. Bunting very angry. Holding the poker firmly, he ran into the room, closely followed by Mrs. Bunting.

"Come on, my dear," and then Mr. Bunting stopped. For the room was perfectly empty.

And yet they knew that they had heard someone moving in the room. They stood still for half a minute. Then Mrs. Bunting went across the room and looked behind the curtain, while Mr. Bunting looked under the desk and up the chimney, and pushed the poker up into the darkness. Then they stood still with eyes questioning each other.

"I was quite sure——" said Mrs. Bunting.

"The candle!" said Mr. Bunting. "Who lit the candle?"

"The drawer!" said Mrs. Bunting. "And the money's gone!"

She went quickly to the doorway.

"Who in the world——"

There was a loud sneeze in the passage. They rushed out, and as they did so the kitchen door slammed![1] "Bring the candle!" said Mr. Bunting, and led the way.

As he opened the kitchen door, he saw that the back door was just opening, and the light of sunrise showed the garden beyond. He was certain that nothing went out of the door. It opened, stood open for a moment, and then closed with a slam.

. . . It was a minute or more before they came back into the kitchen.

The place was empty. They fastened the back door and examined the kitchen and all the rooms thoroughly. There was not a soul to be found in the house, though they searched upstairs and down.

---

[1] Shut with a loud noise.

Daylight found the vicar and his wife still wondering and searching by the unnecessary light of a dying candle.

"Of all the surprising events, this is——" began the vicar for the twentieth time.

"My dear," said Mrs. Bunting, "there's the maid coming down. Just wait here until she has gone into the kitchen, and then go upstairs."

CHAPTER 6

THE FURNITURE THAT WENT MAD

As Hall came downstairs, in the early hours of Whit Monday, he noticed that the stranger's door was open and the front door unfastened. He remembered holding the candle while Mrs. Hall fastened it the night before. At the sight he stopped; then went upstairs again. He knocked at the stranger's door. There was no answer. He knocked again; then pushed the door wide open and entered.

It was as he expected. The bed, the room also, was empty. And what was still more strange, on the bedroom chair and on the bed were scattered the clothes, the only clothes so far as he knew, and the bandages of their guest. His big hat was hanging on the bedpost.

As Hall stood there he heard his wife's voice coming from the cellar.

He turned and hurried down to her.

"Jenny," he said, "he's not in his room and the front door is unfastened."

At first Mrs. Hall did not understand, but as soon as she did she determined to see the empty room for herself. Hall went first. "If he's not there, his clothes are. And what is he doing without his clothes?"

As they went up the cellar steps they both thought they heard the front door open and shut, but, seeing it closed and seeing nothing there, neither said a word to the other about it at the time. Mrs. Hall passed her husband in the passage, and ran on first upstairs. Someone on the staircase sneezed. Hall, following six steps behind, thought that he heard her sneeze; she, going first, thought that Hall was sneezing. She threw open the door and stood looking round the room. "What an extraordinary thing!" she said.

She heard a sniff close behind her, as it seemed, and, turning, was surprised to see Hall some distance away on the top stair. But in another moment he was beside her. She bent forward and put her hand on the pillow and then under the bed-clothes.

"Cold," she said. "He's been up an hour or more."

As she did so, a most unexpected thing happened. The bed-clothes gathered themselves together, jumped up suddenly into a sort of hill, and then jumped headlong off the bed. It was just as if a hand had thrown them aside. Then the stranger's hat jumped off the bedpost, flew through the air, and came straight at Mrs. Hall's face. Then swiftly came the sponge from the washstand, and the chair first threw the stranger's coat and trousers carelessly aside, laughed in a voice very like the stranger's, turned itself up with its four legs pointing at Mrs. Hall, seemed to take aim at her for a moment, and then moved quickly towards her. She screamed and turned, and the chair legs came gently but firmly against her back and pushed her and Hall out of the room. The door slammed, and was locked. The chair and the bed seemed to be dancing for a moment, and then at once everything was still.

Mrs. Hall was left almost fainting in Mr. Hall's arms in the passage. It was with the greatest difficulty that Mr. Hall and Millie, now dressed, succeeded in getting her downstairs.

"Spirits," said Mrs. Hall. "I know it is spirits. I have read about them in the papers. Tables and chairs dancing."

"Lock him out," she went on. "Don't let him come in again. I half guessed . . . I might have known. With those eyes and bandaged head, and never going to church on Sunday. And all those bottles—more than it's right for anyone to have. He's put the spirits into the furniture. . . . My good old furniture! 'Twas in that very chair my poor dear mother used to sit when I was a little girl. To think it should rise up against me now. . . ."

They sent Millie across the street through the golden five o'clock sunshine to wake up Mr. Sandy Wadgers.

He was a clever man, was Mr. Wadgers. "Magic," he said.

C

He came to the inn greatly troubled. They wanted him to lead the way upstairs to the room; but he didn't seem to be in any hurry. He preferred to talk in the passage. Then Mr. Huxter came and joined in the talk. There was a great deal of talking, but nothing was done.

" Let's have the facts first," said Mr. Sandy Wadgers. " Let's be sure we'd be acting perfectly right in breaking that door open."

And suddenly and most wonderfully the door of the room upstairs opened of its own accord, and they saw coming down the stairs the muffled figure of the stranger, staring more blackly than ever through those large spectacles. He came down stiffly and slowly, staring all the time; he walked across the passage, staring, then stopped.

Then he entered the parlour, and suddenly and swiftly shut the door in their faces.

Not a word was spoken until the last echoes of the slam had died away. They stared at one another.

" Well, I've never seen anything like it! " said Mr. Wadgers, more troubled than ever.

" I'd go in and ask him about it," said Wadgers to Mr. Hall. " I'd demand an explanation."

It took some time to get Mr. Hall to do it. At last he knocked, opened the door, and got as far as:

" Excuse me——"

" Go to the devil! " said the stranger, " and shut that door after you."

And that was all.

CHAPTER 7

THE UNVEILING OF THE STRANGER

THE stranger went into the little parlour of the "Coach and Horses" about half-past five in the morning, and there he remained until near midday, the blinds down, the door shut, and nobody went near him.

All that time he could have eaten nothing. Three times he rang his bell, the third time loud and long, but no one answered him. "Telling us to go to the devil, indeed!" said Mrs. Hall. Presently came the story of the robbery at the Vicarage, and that started them thinking. Hall went off with Wadgers to find Mr. Shuckleforth, the magistrate, and take his advice. No one went upstairs, and no one knew what the stranger was doing. Now and then he walked swiftly up and down, and they heard him cursing, tearing paper, breaking bottles.

The little group grew bigger. Mrs. Huxter came over; some young fellows joined them. There was a stream of unanswered questions. Young Archie Harker tried to peep under the drawn curtains. He could see nothing, but others of the Iping youth presently joined him.

And inside in the darkness of the parlour, the stranger, hungry and afraid, hidden in his uncomfortable hot clothes, stared through his dark glasses at his paper, or shook his dirty little bottles or cursed at the boys outside the windows. In the corner by the fireplace lay the pieces of half a dozen broken bottles, and the sharp smell of some gas filled the air.

About noon he suddenly opened his parlour door and stood looking at the three or four people in the bar. "Mrs. Hall," he said. Somebody went and called for her.

She soon appeared, a little short of breath, and so all the more angry. Hall was still out. She had thought it all out before, and had brought the stranger's unpaid bill.

"Why wasn't my breakfast laid?" he asked. "Why haven't you prepared my meals and answered my bell? Do you think I live without eating?"

"Why isn't my bill paid?" said Mrs. Hall. "That's what I want to know."

"I told you three days ago I was expecting some money——"

"I told you three days ago I wasn't going to wait. You can't complain if your breakfast waits a bit, if my bill's been waiting these five days, can you?"

The stranger swore in answer.

"And I'd thank you, sir, if you'd keep your swearing to yourself, sir," said Mrs. Hall.

"Look here, my good woman——" he began.

"Don't call me your good woman," said Mrs. Hall.

"I've told you my money hasn't come."

"Money, indeed!" said Mrs. Hall.

"Still, in my pocket——"

"You told me three days ago that you hadn't anything but a pound's worth of silver upon you."

"Well, I've found some more."

"I wonder where you found it?" said Mrs. Hall.

He stamped his foot. "What do you mean?" he said.

"I mean I wonder where you found it," said Mrs. Hall. "And before I take any bills, or get any breakfasts, or do any such things, you must tell me one or two things that I don't understand, and that nobody understands, and that everybody is very anxious to understand. I want to know what you have been doing to my chair upstairs, and I want to know how it is your room was empty and how you got in again? Those who stop in this house come in by the doors—that's the rule of this house, and that you *didn't* do, and what I want to know is how you *did* come. And I want to know——"

Suddenly the stranger raised his gloved fists, stamped his foot, and said, "Stop!" so loudly that he silenced her at once.

"You don't understand," he said, "who I am or what I am. I'll show you. By heaven! I'll show you." Then he put his open hand over his face and withdrew it. His face became a black hole. "Here," he said. He stepped forward and handed Mrs. Hall something which she, staring at his face, took without thinking. Then, when she saw what it was, she screamed loudly and dropped it. The nose—it was the stranger's nose! pink and shining—rolled on the floor with a sound of hollow cardboard.

Then he removed his spectacles, and everyone in the bar breathed deeply. He took off his hat, and tore at his beard and bandages.

It was worse than anything they had ever seen. Mrs. Hall, open-mouthed with terror, ran to the door of the house.

Everyone began to move. They expected scars, wounds, something ugly, but they saw—*nothing*! The bandages and false hair flew across the passage into the bar. Everyone fell over everyone else down the steps. For the man who stood there shouting was a man up to the shoulders, and then—*nothing*!

People down the village heard shouts, and looking up the street saw the people rushing out of the inn. They saw Mrs. Hall fall down, and Mr. Teddy Henfrey jump, so as not to fall over her, and then they heard the frightful screams of Millie, who, running quickly from the kitchen at the noise, had come upon the headless stranger from behind. Then her screams stopped suddenly.

Everyone in the village street, old and young, about forty or more, collected in a crowd about the inn door.

"What was he doing?"

"Ran at them with a knife."

"I heard the girl scream."

"No head, I tell you."

"Nonsense."

"Took off his bandages."

Everyone spoke at once. Suddenly Mr. Hall appeared, very red and determined, then Mr. Bobby Jaffers, the village policeman, and then the solemn Mr. Wadgers.

Mr. Hall marched up the steps, marched straight to the door of the parlour and found it open.

"Policeman," he said, "do your duty."

Jaffers marched in, Hall next, Wadgers last. They saw the headless figure facing them, with a gnawed crust of bread in one gloved hand and a piece of cheese in the other.

"That's him," said Hall.

"What the devil's this?" came in an angry tone from above the collar of the figure.

"Well, Mister," said Jaffers, "I've got to take you, head or no head."

"Keep off!" said the stranger, jumping back.

He took off his glove and with it struck Jaffers in the face. In another moment Jaffers had gripped him by the handless wrist, and caught his invisible throat. He got a hard kick that made him shout with pain, but he kept his hold. A chair stood in the way, and fell with a crash as they came down together.

"Get hold of his feet," said Jaffers between his teeth to the other men.

When he tried to obey this order, Mr. Hall received a great kick in the ribs that finished him for a time; and Mr. Wadgers, seeing that the headless stranger had rolled over and got on top of Jaffers, went backwards towards the door, and so bumped into Mr. Huxter and another man coming to help the police. Four bottles fell and broke on the floor, filling the room with a powerful smell.

"I give in," said the stranger, though he had thrown Jaffers down and in another moment he stood up, shaking, breathless. A strange thing, he looked, without head or hands. His voice seemed to come out of nothing.

Jaffers also got up.

The stranger ran his arm down his coat, and the buttons to which his empty sleeve pointed became undone. Then he bent down, and seemed to touch his shoes.

"Why!" said Huxter suddenly, "that's not a man at all. It's just empty clothes. Look! You can see down his collar and his clothes. I could put my arm——"

He stretched out his hand; it seemed to meet something in the air, and he drew it back with a sharp cry of surprise. "I

"THE SHIRT SLEEVE PLANTED A BLOW IN HALL'S FACE——"

wish you'd keep your fingers out of my eye," shouted the voice in anger.

"The fact is, I'm all here—head, hands, legs, and all the rest of it, but it happens I'm invisible. But that's no reason why you should put your fingers in my eye, is it?"

The suit of clothes, now all unbuttoned, stood up.

Several other men had now come into the room, so that it was crowded. "Invisible, eh?" said Huxter. "Who ever heard of such a thing?"

"It's strange, perhaps, but it's not a crime. Why am I attacked by a policeman in this way?—"

"Ah! that's different," said Jaffers. "I can't see you, but I have orders to take you in charge not because you can't be seen, but because a house has been robbed."

"Well?"

"And it looks as if——"

"Nonsense," said the Invisible Man.

"I hope so, sir. But I've got my orders."

Suddenly the man sat down, and before anyone could think of stopping him, he had thrown off all his clothes except his shirt.

"Here, stop that," said Jaffers suddenly. "Hold him," he cried. "If he gets his shirt off——"

"Hold him," shouted everyone, and there was a rush at the white shirt, which was now all that could be seen of the stranger.

The shirt sleeve planted a blow in Hall's face that sent him backward into old Toothsome, the grave-digger, and in another moment the shirt was lifted up, just like a shirt that is being pulled over a man's head. Jaffers tore at it, and only helped to pull it off. He was struck in the mouth out of the air, and drew his truncheon[1] and hit Teddy Henfrey hard upon the crown of his head.

"Look out!" said everybody, hitting everywhere at nothing. "Hold him! Shut the door! Don't let him go! I've got something! Here he is!" Everybody was being hit at once,

---

[1] A heavy short stick carried by a policeman.

falling on one another. Sandy Wadgers opened the door and they fell out. The hitting went on. One man had a tooth broken, another a swollen ear. Jaffers was struck under the jaw. He caught at something hard that stood between him and Huxter. Then the whole mass of struggling, excited men fell out into the crowded hall.

The battle moved swiftly to the house door. There were excited cries of "Hold him!" "Invisible!" and so on, and a young fellow, a stranger to the place, rushed in at once, caught something, missed his hold, and fell over a man's body. Half-way across the road a woman screamed as something pushed by her, a dog ran howling into Huxter's yard, and with that the Invisible Man was gone.

For a moment people stood, not knowing what to do. And then they ran, scattered as the wind scatters dead leaves. But Jaffers lay quite still, face and knees bent upwards by the steps of the inn.

CHAPTER 8

ON THE ROAD

Mr. Thomas Marvel, a tramp,[1] had removed his boots and sat by the roadside cooling his feet and pitifully looking at his toes. They were the best boots he had worn for a long time, yet he hated them for their ugliness and their size. "The ugliest boots in the whole world, I should think," he said.

"They're boots, anyhow," said a Voice.

"Yes," Mr. Marvel agreed, " I had them given to me. Too large. I'm tired of them. That's why I've been begging for boots, boots, boots everywhere, but no one has any to give away."

"H'm," said the Voice.

"No. I have been begging for boots round here for ten years, got all my boots about here, and now look at them, they're the best they can do for me."

He turned his head over his shoulder to look at the boots of the speaker—and they weren't there. There were neither boots nor legs—nothing.

"Where are you? " he asked. He saw the road, the open country, but no sign of any man but himself.

"Am I mad? I must be seeing things."

"No, you are not," said the Voice. "Don't be frightened."

"Frightened, frightened! " said Mr. Marvel. "Come here. Where are you? "

"Don't be frightened," said the Voice.

"You'll be frightened soon. Let me get hold of you. Are you buried? "

There was no answer.

Mr. Marvel began to put on his coat.

[1] A poor man who walks from place to place.

" I could have sworn I heard a voice."

" So you did."

" It's there again," said Mr. Marvel, closing his eyes and drawing his hand across his forehead. " I must have gone mad."

" Don't be a fool," said the Voice.

" I——"

" One minute," said the Voice. " You think I'm just imagination—just imagination? "

" What else can you be? " said Mr. Marvel, rubbing the back of his neck.

" Very well," said the Voice, " I'm going to throw stones at you till you think differently."

" But where are you? "

The Voice made no answer. Whizz came a stone, as it seemed out of the air, and just missed Mr. Marvel's shoulder. He turned round and saw a stone jump up into the air, stand a moment and fall at his feet. Another came and hit his bare toes, which made Mr. Marvel cry aloud. Then he started to run, fell over something unseen, and came to rest sitting by the road.

" *Now*," said the Voice, " am I just imagination? "

Mr. Marvel struggled to his feet, and was immediately rolled over again. He lay quiet for a moment.

" If you struggle any more," said the Voice, " I shall throw this stone at your head."

" I am finished," said Mr. Thomas Marvel, sitting up, taking his wounded toe in his hand. " I don't understand it. Stones throwing themselves. Stones talking. I'm finished."

" It's very simple," said the Voice. " I'm an invisible man."

" Tell me something I don't know," said Mr. Marvel groaning with pain. " Where you're hidden—how you do it—I *don't* know. I'm beaten."

" I'm invisible," said the Voice. " That's what I want you to understand."

" Anyone can see that. There is no need for you to be so angry. *Now*, then. Give us an idea. Where are you hidden? "

" I'm invisible. That's the point. And what **I want you** to understand is this——"

" But where are you? " interrupted Mr. Marvel.

" Here—six yards in front of you."

" Oh, no! I'm not blind. You'll be telling me **next you're** just thin air."

" Yes. I am—thin air. You're looking through me."

" What! Isn't there anything in you? "

" I am just a human being—solid, needing food **and drink,** needing clothes, too. . . . But I'm invisible. You see? Invisible. Simple idea. Invisible."

" What, are you real? "

" Yes, real."

" Let me feel your hand," said Marvel, " if you *are* real. It won't be so strange."

He felt with his fingers the hand that had closed round his wrist and his touch went up the arm, patted a chest, and touched a bearded face.

Mr. Marvel's face showed complete astonishment.

" Of course, all this isn't half so wonderful as you think," said the Invisible Man.

" It's quite wonderful enough for me," said Mr. Thomas Marvel. " How do you manage it? How is it done? "

" It's a very long story. And besides——"

" I tell you, the whole business is—I can't understand," said Mr. Marvel.

" What I want to say now is this: I need help. I have come to that. I came upon you suddenly. I was wandering, naked, helpless. And I saw you——"

" Oh, *Lord*! " said Mr. Marvel.

" I came up behind you—stopped—went on. Then stopped. ' Here,' I said to myself, ' is the man for me.' So I turned and came back to you. You. And——"

" Oh, *Lord*! " said Mr. Marvel. " May I ask: How is it?—and what may you be requiring in the way of help? Invisible! "

" I want you to help me get clothes and shelter, and then

other things. I've left those things long enough. If you won't
—well! . . . But you *will*—you *must*."

"Look here," said Mr. Marvel. "Don't knock me about
any more. And let me go. I must get steady a bit. And
you've pretty near broken my toe. It's all so unreasonable.
Empty earth, empty sky. Nothing visible for miles except
Nature. And then comes a voice. A voice out of heaven!
And stones. And a fist. Lord!"

"Pull yourself together," said the Voice, "for you have to
do the work I want you to do."

Mr. Marvel blew out his cheeks, and his eyes were round.

"I've chosen you," said the Voice. "You are the only man,
except some of those fools down there, who know there is
such a thing as an Invisible Man. You have to be my helper.
Help me—and I will do great things for you. An Invisible
Man is a man of great power." He stopped for a moment to
sneeze loudly.

"But if you betray me," he said, "if you fail to do as I tell
you——"

He paused and tapped Mr. Marvel's shoulder sharply. Mr.
Marvel gave a cry of terror at the touch. "I don't want to
betray you," said Mr. Marvel, moving away from the fingers.
"Don't you think that, whatever you do. All I want to do is
help you—just tell me what I have got to do. . . . Whatever
you want done, I'm most willing to do it."

About four o'clock Mr. Marvel entered the village from the
direction of the hills. He was a short, stout person in a shabby
old hat, and he seemed to be very much out of breath. There
was fear in his face, and he seemed to be talking to himself.
Some of the village men remember seeing him. Mr. Huxter
saw him go up the steps of the inn, and turn towards the
parlour. Mr. Huxter heard voices from the parlour telling the
man that he must not go in.

"That room's private!" said Hall, and Mr. Marvel shut the
door and went into the bar.

Later he came out again, wiping his mouth as if he had been
having a drink.

CHAPTER 9

IN THE "COACH AND HORSES"

MR. CUSS and Mr. Bunting were in the parlour of the inn, searching the stranger's property in the hope of finding something to explain the events of the morning. Jaffers had recovered from his fall and had gone home. Mrs. Hall had tidied the stranger's clothes and put them away. And under the window where the stranger did his work, Mr. Cuss found three big books—a Diary.

"Now," said Cuss, "we shall learn something."

But when they opened the books they could read nothing. Cuss turned the pages.

"Dear me," he said, "I can't understand."

"No pictures, nothing to show——?" asked Mr. Bunting.

"See for yourself," said Mr. Cuss, "it is all Greek or Russian or some other language."

The door opened suddenly. Both men looked round. It was Mr. Marvel. He held the door open for a moment.

"I beg pardon," he said.

"Please shut that door," said Mr. Cuss, and Mr. Marvel went out.

"My nerves—my nerves are all wrong to-day," said Mr. Cuss. "It made me jump, the door opening like that."

Mr. Bunting smiled. "Now let us look at the books. . . . It is certain that strange things have been happening in the village. But, of course, I can't believe in an Invisible Man. I can't . . ."

"No. Yet I tell you I saw right down his sleeve."

"But are you sure?" said Mr. Bunting. "Are you quite sure?"

"Quite. I've said so. There's no doubt at all. Now the books."

They turned over the pages, unable to read a word of their strange language. Suddenly Mr. Bunting felt something take hold of the back of his neck. He was unable to lift his head.

"Don't move, little men, or I'll brain you both."

Mr. Bunting looked at Cuss, whose face had turned white and sickly.

"I am sorry to be rough," said the Voice. "Since when did you learn to interfere with other men's goods?"

Two chins struck the table. "To come unasked into a stranger's private room! Listen. I am a strong man. I could kill you both and escape unseen, if I wanted to. If I let you go you must promise to do as I tell you."

"Yes," said Mr. Bunting.

Then the hands let their necks go and the two men sat up, now very red in the face.

"Don't move," said the Voice. "Here's the poker, you see."

They saw the poker dance in the air. It touched Mr. Bunting's nose.

"Now, where are my clothes? Just at present, though the days are quite warm enough for an invisible man to run about naked—the evenings are cold. I want some clothes. And I must also have those three books."

CHAPTER 10

THE INVISIBLE MAN LOSES HIS TEMPER

WHILE these things were going on in the parlour, and while Mr. Huxter was watching Mr. Marvel as he leaned smoking his pipe against the gate, a few yards away stood Mr. Hall and Teddy Henfrey talking.

Suddenly there came a loud knock on the door of the parlour, a cry, and then—silence.

" *Hul*-lo! " said Teddy Henfrey.

" *Hul*-lo! " from the bar.

Mr. Hall and Teddy looked at the door.

" Something wrong," said Hall.

For a long time they listened. Strange noises were coming from behind the closed door, as if something was falling about. Then a sharp cry.

" No! No, you don't." Then silence.

" What is that? " exclaimed Henfrey in a low voice.

" Is all right there? " asked Hall.

" Quite ri-ight," came Mr. Bunting's voice, " qui-ite! D-don't come in."

They stood listening.

" I can't," they heard Mr. Bunting say; " I tell you, sir, I will not."

" Who's that speaking now? " asked Henfrey.

" Mr. Cuss, I s'pose," said Hall. " Can you hear anything? " Silence.

" Sounds like throwing the table about," said Hall.

Mrs. Hall appeared behind the bar. When they told her, she would not believe anything strange was happening. Perhaps they were moving the chairs and table.

" Didn't I hear the window? " said Mr. Henfrey.

" What window? " asked Mrs. Hall.

48

"Parlour window," said Henfrey.

Everyone stood listening. Mrs. Hall's eyes, looking straight before her, saw, without seeing, the bright oblong of the inn door, the white road, and Huxter's shop-front shining in the June sun. Suddenly Huxter's door opened, and Huxter appeared, eyes staring with excitement, arms waving.

"Stop thief!" cried Huxter, and he ran towards the yard gates and disappeared.

At the same time came a noise from the parlour, and the sound of windows being closed.

Hall, Henfrey, and everyone in the bar rushed out at once into the street. They saw someone run round the corner towards the hill road, and Mr. Huxter leap into the air and fall on his face and shoulder. Hall and two workmen ran down the street and saw Mr. Marvel disappearing past the church wall.

But Hall had hardly run twelve yards when he gave a loud shout and fell on his side, pulling one of the workmen with him. The second workman came up, and he too was knocked down. Then came the rush of the village crowd. The first man was surprised to see Huxter and Hall on the ground. Suddenly something happened to his feet, and he was lying on his back, the crowd was falling over him, and he was being cursed by a number of angry people.

Now, when Hall and Henfrey and the workmen ran out of the house, Mrs. Hall had remained in the bar. Suddenly the parlour door was opened, Mr. Cuss appeared, and, without looking at her, rushed at once down the steps towards the corner of the street. "Hold him!" he cried, "don't let him drop those books! You can see him so long as he holds those books."

He knew nothing of Marvel; for the Invisible Man had handed over the books to him in the yard. The face of Mr. Cuss was angry and determined, but there was something wrong with his clothes: he was wearing a tablecloth. "Hold him!" he shouted. "He's got my trousers!—and all the vicar's clothes!"

D

Coming round the corner to join the crowd, he was knocked off his feet and lay kicking on the ground. Somebody trod on his finger. He struggled to his feet, something knocked against him and threw him on all fours again, and he saw that everyone was running back to the village. He rose again, and was hit behind the ear. He set off straight back to the village inn as fast as he could run, and on his way leapt over the deserted Huxter, who was now sitting up.

Behind him, as he was half-way up the inn steps, he heard a sudden cry of anger above the noise, and a sounding smack in someone's face. He knew the voice as that of the Invisible Man.

In another moment Mr. Cuss was back in the parlour.

"He's coming back, Bunting!" he said, rushing in. "Save yourself!"

Mr. Bunting was standing in the window, trying to clothe himself in the carpet and a newspaper.

"Who's coming?" he said, so surprised that his dress nearly fell off him.

"Invisible Man!" said Cuss, and rushed to the window. "We'd better move—quick. He's fighting mad. Mad!"

In another moment he was out in the yard.

Mr. Bunting heard a frightful struggle in the passage of the inn, and decided to go. He climbed out of the window, and ran up the village street as fast as his fat little legs could carry him.

" ' I SHALL KEEP MY HAND ON YOUR SHOULDER,' SAID THE VOICE "

CHAPTER 11

MR. MARVEL TRIES TO SAY NO

MR. MARVEL was walking painfully behind the beech woods on the road to Bramblehurst. He looked very unhappy and was carrying three books and some clothes wrapped in a blue tablecloth. A Voice went with him: he was held fast by unseen hands.

" If you try to escape again—if you try to escape again," said the Voice, " I will kill you."

" I didn't try to escape," said Mr. Marvel.

The Voice broke into curses and then ceased. Mr. Marvel, who was not accustomed to so much work, was worn out. There was silence for a time. Then, " I shall have to make use of you. You are a poor creature, but I must."

" Yes, I am," said Marvel.

" You are," said the Voice.

" I'm not strong," said Marvel. Then after a short silence he repeated, " I'm not strong. I've got a weak heart. I can't do what you want."

" I'll make you," said the Voice.

" I wish I was dead," said Marvel.

" Go on! Walk! Move! " said the Voice.

" It's cruel," said Marvel.

" Be quiet," said the Voice. " I will see that you are all right. But be quiet. I want to think."

Soon they saw the lights of a village.

" I shall keep my hand on your shoulder," said the Voice. " Go straight through the village, and do not try to say anything to anybody."

CHAPTER 12

AT PORT STOWE

At ten o'clock the next morning Mr. Marvel, dirty, sad, almost ready to weep, sat outside a little inn at Port Stowe. Beside him were the books, but now they were tied up with string. He had left the clothes in the woods beyond Bramblehurst. Mr. Marvel sat on the bench, and although no one took any notice of him, he seemed excited.

When he had been sitting for nearly an hour, however, an old sailor, with a newspaper in his hand, came out of the inn and sat down beside him.

"Pleasant day," said the sailor.

Mr. Marvel looked about him with something very like terror. "Very," he said.

The sailor looked about him as if he had nothing to do, and then at Mr. Marvel's dusty clothes and the books beside him. He had heard the sound of money being dropped into a pocket, and thought that Mr. Marvel did not look like a man to carry much money.

"Books?" he said suddenly.

Mr. Marvel jumped and looked at them. "Oh, yes," he said. "Yes, they're books."

"There are some strange things in books," said the sailor.

"There are," said Mr. Marvel.

"And some strange things out of them," said the sailor.

"True," said Mr. Marvel.

"There are some strange things in newspapers, for example," said the sailor.

"There are."

"In *this* newspaper," said the sailor.

"Ah!" said Mr. Marvel.

"There's a story," said the sailor, "there's a story about an Invisible Man." And with that he told Mr. Marvel as much of the story as the newspaper contained.

"I don't like it," he said. "He might be anywhere, might be here at this moment listening to us. And just think, if he wanted to steal or kill, what is there to stop him?"

Mr. Marvel seemed to be listening for the least sound.

"Ah—and—well . . ." he said. And lowering his voice, "I happen to know something about this Invisible Man."

"Oh," said the sailor, "you?"

"Yes," said Mr. Marvel, "me."

The sailor did not seem to believe Mr. Marvel.

"It happened like this," Mr. Marvel began, and then his expression changed suddenly.

"Ow!" he said. He rose stiffly from his seat, as if in pain. "Wow!" he said.

"What's the matter?" said the sailor.

"I—I think I must be going," said Mr. Marvel.

"But you were just going to tell me about this Invisible Man," said the sailor.

Mr. Marvel seemed to think carefully.

"A lie," said a Voice.

"It's a lie," said Mr. Marvel.

"But it's in the paper," said the sailor.

"Yes," said Mr. Marvel loudly, "but it's a lie. I know the man who started it. There isn't any Invisible Man whatsoever. . . ."

"But this paper? D'you mean to say——?"

"Not a word of truth in it," said Mr. Marvel firmly.

The sailor stared, paper in hand. Mr. Marvel turned round.

"Wait a bit," said the sailor, rising and speaking slowly. "D'you mean to say——?"

"I do," said Mr. Marvel.

"Then why did you let me go on and tell you all this, then? What do you mean by letting a man make a fool of himself like that for, eh?"

"Come along," said a Voice, and Mr. Marvel was suddenly

turned round about and started marching off in a strange, jumpy manner.

"Silly devil," said the sailor, legs wide apart, watching the little man go. "I'll show you, you silly fool! It's here in the paper!"

And there was another strange thing he was soon to hear that had happened quite close to him. And that was a "fist full of money" (no less) travelling of its own accord along by the wall. A sailor friend had seen this wonderful sight that very morning. He had tried to take the money and had been knocked down by an unseen hand, and when he had got to his feet the money had disappeared.

The story of the flying money was true. And all round that neighbourhood, even from the bank, from shops and inns, money had quietly walked away. And it had found its way into Mr. Marvel's pocket, so the sailor had heard.

CHAPTER 13

THE MAN IN A HURRY

In the early evening time Dr. Kemp was sitting in his study on the hill above Burdock. It was a pleasant little upstairs room, with three windows—north, west, and south—with bookshelves crowded with books and with a broad writing-table. Dr. Kemp was a tall, thin man of about thirty-five, with little left of his once thick fair hair. He was writing.

And his eye, presently wandering from his work, caught the sunset at the back of the hill opposite his house. For a minute, perhaps, he sat, pen in mouth, admiring the rich golden colour, and then he saw the little figure of a man running over the hill towards him. He was a shortish little fellow, in a shabby old hat, and he was running fast.

Dr. Kemp got up, went to the window, and stared at the hillside and the dark little figure running down it. "He seems in a hurry," said Dr. Kemp.

Then the running man was hidden behind some houses; he came into sight and disappeared again—still running.

But those who saw him nearer, saw the terror in his face. He looked neither to the right nor left, but his wide eyes stared straight down the hill to where the lamps were being lit and the people were crowded in the street. Everybody he passed stopped and began staring up and down the road, and asking one another, half afraid, why the man was running so hard.

And then presently, far up the hill, a dog playing in the road howled and ran under a gate, and as they still wondered, something—a wind—a noise of feet, a sound like heavy breathing, rushed by.

People screamed. People sprang off the foot-walk. They

shouted as the thing rushed past them down the hill, they were still shouting in the street before Marvel was half-way there. They were running into houses with the news and shutting the doors behind them. He heard it, and made one last rush. Fear came striding[1] by, rushed ahead of him, and in a moment had seized the town.

"The Invisible Man is coming! *The Invisible Man!*"

[1] Running or walking with long steps.

CHAPTER 14

IN THE " JOLLY CRICKETERS "

THE " Jolly Cricketers " is an inn just at the bottom of the hill. The barman[1] leant his fat red arms on the counter and talked about horses with a cabman, while a black-bearded man who spoke like an American, ate biscuits and cheese, and talked to a policeman.

" What's the shouting about? " said the cabman, trying to see up the hill over the dirty yellow curtains in the low window of the inn. Somebody ran past outside.

" Fire, perhaps," said the barman.

The door was pushed open, and Marvel, weeping, his hat gone, the neck of his coat torn open, rushed in, and tried to shut the door. It was held half open by a strap.

" Coming! " he cried, his voice cracked with terror. " He's coming. The Invisible Man! After me. For God's sake. Help! Help! Help! "

" Shut the doors," said the policeman. " Who's coming? What's the matter? " He went to the door, released the strap, and the door slammed. The man with the beard closed the other door.

" Let me hide," said Marvel, weeping. " Let me hide. Lock me in—somewhere. I tell you he's after me. I escaped. He said he'd kill me, and he will."

" *You're* safe," said the man with the black beard. " The door's shut. What's it all about? "

" Let me hide," said Marvel, and cried aloud as a blow suddenly made the fastened door shake. The blow was followed by a hurried knocking and a shouting outside.

" Hullo," cried the policeman, " who's there? "

[1] A man who serves people with drink in the bar of an inn.

58

"He'll kill me," shouted Mr. Marvel, "he's got a knife or something. Don't open the door. *Please* don't open the door. *Where* shall I hide?"

"Is this the Invisible Man, then?" asked the black-bearded man with one hand behind him. "I guess it's about time we saw him."

The window of the inn was suddenly broken in, and there were screams and a running to and fro in the street. The policeman had been standing on a bench looking out of the window to see who was at the door. He got down. "That's what it is," he said. The barman stood in front of the bar-parlour door, which was now locked on Mr. Marvel, stared at the broken window, and came round to the two other men.

Everything was suddenly quiet. "I wish I had my truncheon," said the policeman, going to the door. "Once we open, in he comes. There's no stopping him."

"Don't you be in too much of a hurry about that door," said the cabman anxiously.

"Unfasten it," said the man with the black beard, "and if he comes . . ." He showed a gun in his hand.

"That won't do," said the policeman, "that's murder."

"I know what country I'm in," said the man with the beard. "I'm going to shoot at his legs. Unfasten it."

"Not with that thing going off behind me," said the barman.

"Very well," said the man with the black beard. He stooped down, gun ready, and drew the bolts himself. Barman, cabman and policeman turned about.

"Come in," said the bearded man in a low voice, standing back and facing the doors with his gun behind him. No one came in, the door remained closed.

Five minutes afterwards, "Are all the doors of the house shut?" asked Marvel. "He's going round to the back."

"There's the yard door," said the barman, "and the private door. The yard door——"

He rushed out of the bar.

In a minute he appeared again with a carving-knife in his hand. "The yard door was open," he said.

" He may be in the house now," said the cabman.

The man with the beard put the gun back in his pocket. And even as he did so, the catch of the door broke and the bar-parlour door burst open. They heard Marvel squeal and ran to his rescue. The bearded man's pistol cracked, and the looking-glass at the back of the parlour came smashing and tinkling down.

As the barman came into the room, he saw Marvel struggling against the door that led to the yard and kitchen. The door flew open and Marvel was dragged into the kitchen.

The policeman, who had been trying to pass the barman, rushed in, followed by the cabman, caught hold of the invisible hand that held Marvel, was hit in the face and went down. Then the cabman clutched something.

" I've got him," said the cabman.

" Here he is ! " said the barman.

Mr. Marvel suddenly dropped to the ground, and made an attempt to crawl behind the legs of the fighting men. The struggle went backwards and forwards about the door. The voice of the Invisible Man was heard for the first time, as the policeman trod on his foot. Then he cried out, and his fists flew round. The cabman suddenly cried and fell, with a kick in the stomach. The doors into the bar-parlour from the kitchen slammed and covered Mr. Marvel's retreat.[1] The men in the kitchen found themselves struggling with empty air.

" Where's he gone? " cried the man with the beard. " Out? "

" This way," said the policeman, stepping into the yard and stopping.

A large stone flew by his head and fell on the kitchen table.

" I'll show him," shouted the man with the black beard, and suddenly five bullets from his gun had followed one another in the direction the stone had come from. As he fired, the man with the beard moved his hand a little, so that his shots went from one side to the other of the narrow yard.

A silence followed. " Come along," he said, " and feel about for his body."

[1] Running away

CHAPTER 15

DR. KEMP'S VISITOR

DR. KEMP was writing in his study when he heard the shots. Crack, crack, crack, they came one after the other.

"Hullo!" said Dr. Kemp, putting his pen into his mouth again and listening. "Who's letting off guns in Burdock? What are they doing now?"

He went to the south window, threw it up, and leaning out stared down on the town. "Looks like a crowd down the hill," he said, "by 'The Cricketers'." Thence his eyes wandered over the town to far away where the ships' lights shone. The moon in its first quarter hung over the hill to the west, and the stars were clear and bright.

Five minutes later, Dr. Kemp pulled down the window again, and returned to his writing-desk.

It must have been about an hour after this that the front-door bell rang. He sat listening. He heard the servant go to the door, and waited for the sound of her feet on the staircase, but she did not come.

"I wonder what that was?" said Dr. Kemp.

He tried to go on with his work, failed, got up, went downstairs from his study, rang the bell, and called to the maid as she appeared in the hall below.

"Was that a letter?" he asked.

"Only the bell ringing, sir, and no one there," she answered.

"I'm restless to-night," he said to himself. He went back to his study.

In a little while he was hard at work again, and his room about him was silent except for the ticking of the clock and the sound of his pen moving over the paper.

It was two o'clock before Dr. Kemp had finished his work for the night. He rose and went upstairs to bed. When he had taken off his coat and vest, he felt thirsty. He took a candle and went down to the dining-room in search of whisky.

Dr. Kemp's scientific work had made him a very observant man. As he crossed the hall he saw a dark spot on the floor near the stairs. He went on upstairs, and then he suddenly wondered what the dark spot on the floor might be. He went back to the hall, and, bending down, touched the spot. He found it had the stickiness and colour of drying blood.

He returned upstairs looking about him and thinking about the blood spot. On the landing he saw something which made him stop. There was blood on the handle of his door.

He looked at his own hand. It was quite clean, and then he remembered that the door of his room had been open when he came down from his study, and that he had not touched the handle at all. He went straight into his bedroom, his face quite calm—perhaps a little more determined than usual. . . . He looked at the bed. There was a mess of blood, and the sheet had been torn. He had not noticed this when he had been in the room before. The other side of the bed looked as if someone had been lying on it.

Then he seemed to hear a low voice say, "Good heavens! —Kemp!" But Dr. Kemp did not believe in "voices".

He stood staring at the sheets. Was it really a voice? He looked about again, but noticed nothing. But he distinctly heard something move across the room. A strange feeling came over him. He closed the door of the room and came forward. Suddenly, with a start, he saw a blood-stained bandage hanging in mid-air between him and the bed.

He stared at it in surprise. It was an empty bandage—a bandage properly tied, but quite empty. He would have advanced to grasp it, but a touch stopped him and a voice spoke quite close to him.

"Kemp!" said the Voice.

"Eh!" said Kemp, with his mouth open.

Said the Voice, "I'm an Invisible Man."

Kemp made no answer for a moment or two, but simply

stared at the bandage. Then "The Invisible Man?" he said.

"I am an Invisible Man," repeated the Voice.

"I thought it was a lie," he said. "Have you a bandage on?" he asked.

"Yes," said the Invisible Man.

"Oh!" said Kemp, and then, "I say!" he said. "But this is nonsense. It's some trick." He stepped forward suddenly, stretched out his hand towards the bandage and met invisible fingers.

"Keep steady, Kemp, for God's sake! I want help badly. Stop!"

The hand gripped his arm. He struck at it. "Kemp!" cried the Voice. "Kemp, keep steady!"

A longing to free himself took hold of Kemp. The hand held his shoulder, and he was suddenly tripped and thrown backwards upon the bed. He opened his mouth to shout, and the corner of the sheet was pushed between his teeth. The Invisible Man had him down, but his arms were free, and he struck and tried to kick savagely.

"Listen to reason, will you?" said the Invisible Man. "By heaven, you'll make me mad!"

"Lie still. Lie still!" said the Invisible Man in Kemp's ear.

Kemp struggled for another moment, and then lay still.

"Let me get up," he said. "I'll stop where I am. And let me sit quiet for a minute."

He sat up and felt his neck.

"I am just an ordinary man—a man you used to know— made invisible. Do you remember Griffin?"

"Griffin?" said Kemp.

"Griffin," answered the Voice. "A younger student than you were."

"What has this to do with Griffin?"

"I *am* Griffin."

Kemp thought. "It's too much of a shock," he said. "But what devilry must happen to make a man invisible?"

"It's no devilry. It's sane and simple enough."

"It's terrible!" said Kemp. "How on earth——?"

"I'm wounded and in pain, and tired. . . . Great God! Kemp, you are a man. Take it steady. Give me some food and drink, and let me sit down here."

Kemp stared at the bandage as it moved across the room, then saw a chair dragged along the floor and come to rest near the bed. It creaked, and the seat sank a quarter of an inch or so. He rubbed his eyes and felt his neck again. "This beats ghosts," he said, and laughed stupidly.

"That's better. Thank heaven, you're getting sensible!"

"Or silly," said Kemp, and rubbed his eyes.

"Give me some whisky. I'm nearly dead."

"It didn't feel like that. Where are you? If I get up shall I run into you? *There!* All right. Whisky. . . . Here. Where shall I give it you?"

Kemp felt the glass taken out of his hand. He let it go into the air. It came to rest twenty inches from the front of the chair-seat. He stared at it.

"This. . . . I don't believe it. . . . I must be mad."

"Nonsense!" said the Voice. "Listen to me. I'm starving, and the night is cold to a naked man."

"Food?" said Kemp.

The glass of whisky tilted itself. "Yes," said the Invisible Man, putting it down. "Can you give me something to wear?"

Kemp found some clothes. "These?" he asked.

They were taken from him. They hung in the air, buttoned themselves and sat down in the chair.

"The maddest thing I've ever seen in my life," said Kemp. "Some food?"

Kemp went to the kitchen for some bread and some meat, returned and put them on a table in front of his guest.

"Never mind about a knife," said the Invisible Man: and a piece of meat hung in the air and disappeared with a sound of eating.

"I always like to have clothes on when I eat," said the Voice.

"Is your arm all right?"

"Not very painful."

"THE GLASS OF WHISKY TILTED ITSELF"

E

"It's all mad, as mad can be."

"Quite reasonable," said the Invisible Man.

"But how's it done?" began Kemp. "What were the shots?" he asked. "How did the shooting begin?"

"There was a man—I tried to make him help me, curse him!—who tried to steal my money. And he has stolen it."

"Is he invisible, too?"

"No."

"Well?"

"Can't I have some more to eat before I tell you all about it? I'm hungry—in pain. And you want me to tell stories!"

Kemp got up. "*You* didn't do any shooting?" he asked.

"Not me," said his visitor. "Some fool fired, a man I'd never seen before. A lot of them got frightened. They all got frightened at me. Curse them! I say—I want more to eat than this, Kemp."

"I'll see whether there's anything more to eat downstairs," said Kemp. "Not much, I'm afraid."

Kemp found some more food. And when his guest had eaten, he told him to try to get some sleep.

CHAPTER 16

THE INVISIBLE MAN SLEEPS

EXHAUSTED and wounded though the Invisible Man was, he refused to accept Kemp's word that no one would try to seize him. He examined the two windows of the bedroom, drew up the blinds and opened the windows to see whether it was possible to get out that way, as Kemp had told him. Outside the night was very quiet and still, and the new moon was setting over the down. Then he examined the keys of the bedroom and the two dressing-room doors. Finally he said he was satisfied. He stood on the hearthrug and Kemp heard the sound of a yawn.

" I'm sorry," said the Invisible Man, " if I cannot tell you all that I've done to-night. But I am worn out. It's foolish, no doubt. It's horrible! But, believe me, Kemp, in spite of your arguments, it is quite a possible thing. I have made a discovery. I meant to keep it secret. I can't. I must have a partner. And you . . . We can do such great things together. . . . But to-morrow. Now, Kemp, I feel as though I must sleep or die."

CHAPTER 17

CERTAIN FIRST PRINCIPLES

THE next morning Kemp heard a loud noise and went to call his guest.

"What's the matter?" asked Kemp, when the Invisible Man admitted him.

"Nothing," was the answer.

"But, confound it! The smash?"

"Fit of temper," said the Invisible Man. "Forgot this arm; and it's sore."

"You're rather liable to that sort of thing."

"I am."

"All your story is in the papers," Kemp said.

The Invisible Man cursed.

"Come and have some breakfast," said Kemp.

"Before we can do anything else," he went on, "I must understand a little more about you." He had sat down, with the air of a man who means to talk seriously.

"It's simple enough," said Griffin.

"No doubt it's simple enough to you, but——" Kemp laughed.

"Well, yes, to me it seemed wonderful at first, no doubt. But we'll do great things yet! I found the stuff first at Chesilstowe College."

"Chesilstowe?"

"I went there after I left London. You know I have always been interested in Light."

"Ah!"

"I said: 'I will devote my life to this. This is worth while.' You know what fools we are at two-and-twenty?"

"Fools then and fools now," said Kemp.

"As though just knowing could satisfy a man!

"I saw a way to change the human body, or any other kind of body. . . ." And then the strange man, or rather the clothes of a man, sitting opposite to Kemp, explained how a student of science had disappeared. It was a long explanation. He began by reminding Kemp how, if you take a small piece of glass and crush it into powder, the powder is white and solid like salt. You cannot see through it. Human flesh, white paper, linen, hair, are really made of a kind of powder. The tiny grains of powder break up the light which shines *upon* them, so that it cannot shine *through* them, and that is why we can see flesh and paper. Now, if you could smooth the broken grains of powder so that they would not break up the light, they would no longer look solid. The light would shine through them, just as now the sun is shining through me. You can try it with a piece of white paper and a drop of oil. Drop a little oil on the paper and things will begin to show through it. If the oil is good enough and the paper is bad enough, you will be able to see through the paper to the print on the other side. That is because the oil is smooth and it smoothes out the rough surfaces of each little grain of the powder.

"Well, I found something which would do to human flesh what the oil does to the paper, and would do it so perfectly, that there is no tiny particle of my body which holds up the light. It is as if you had taken powdered glass and turned it back into unbroken glass of that window—that, only more so."

The explanation, as between two scientists, went on into all kinds of questions. Kemp was so lost in wonder at the story that he nearly forgot that his friend was invisible.

"Yes," said the Voice, "I had found it all. The way was open—and then—then after years of care and secret working —then I knew that I could do nothing. I knew, and I was helpless. And that was after three years of secrecy and trouble."

" Why could you do nothing? " asked Kemp.

" I had no money," said the Invisible Man, and went again to stare out of the window.

He turned round. " I robbed the old man—robbed my father. The money was not his, and he shot himself."

CHAPTER 18

AT THE HOUSE IN GREAT PORTLAND STREET

FOR a moment Kemp sat in silence, staring at the back of the headless figure at the window. Then he rose, took the Invisible Man's arm and turned him away from the view.

"You are tired," he said, "and while I'm sitting down you walk about. Have my chair."

He got up and stood between Griffin and the nearest window.

For a time Griffin sat silent, and then he went on with his story.

"I had already left the College," he said, "when that happened. It was last December. I had taken a room in London, a large empty room in a big lodging-house.

"It was all like a dream, that short visit to my father in my old home. When I came back to my room it seemed like waking from a dream to real things. Here were the things I knew and loved. Here stood the apparatus,[1] the experiments arranged and waiting. And now there was scarcely any difficulty left, beyond the planning of details.

"I will tell you, Kemp, sooner or later, all the complicated processes. We need not talk about that now. For the most part, except certain words I chose to remember, they are written in cipher[2] in those books that that tramp has hidden. We must hunt him down.

"First I tried some white wool. It was the strangest thing in the world to see it fade like smoke and disappear.

"I could scarcely believe I had done it. I put my hand into the emptiness and there was the thing as solid as ever. I felt it, and threw it on the floor. I had a little trouble finding it again.

[1] Things used by men to make experiments in science.
[2] Secret writing.

71

"And then I heard a noise behind me, and, turning, saw a white cat, very dirty, outside the window. A thought came into my head. 'Everything is ready for you,' I said, and went to the window, opened it, and called softly. She came in. The poor beast was starving and I gave her some milk. After that she went smelling round the room, evidently with the idea of making herself at home. The invisible wool upset her a bit; you should have seen her spit at it! But I made her comfortable on my bed."

"And then you made the cat invisible?"

"Yes: it took four hours."

"You don't mean to say there's an Invisible Cat in the world?" said Kemp.

"If it hasn't been killed," said the Invisible Man. "Why not?"

"Why not?" said Kemp. "Go on."

He was silent for a few minutes, then, "My only clear thought," he said, "was that the thing had to be completed. And it must be done soon, for I had little money left. After a time I went home, ate some food and went to sleep in my clothes on my bed. . . .

"There was someone knocking at the door. It was my landlord. He said I had been hurting a cat in the night, he was sure. He wanted to know all about it. I told him there had been no cat in my room. Then the noise of the apparatus could be heard all over the house, he said. That was true, certainly. He came into the room, asked me what I was doing, and said it had always been a respectable house. At last I got angry, pushed him out and shut the door. He made some noise outside, but I did not listen. After a time he went away.

"But I did not know what he meant to do, nor even what he had the power to do. To move to fresh rooms would have meant delay—I had twenty pounds left in the world, most of it in a bank. There would be an inquiry, my room would be searched. What could I do?

"Disappear! Of course. . . . It was all done that evening and night.

"There was some pain at first. I felt sick. At times I sobbed and sobbed. I talked aloud to myself. But I did not give up. I shall never forget seeing my hands. They became white as white paper, and then, slowly, became like glass. And then—they had disappeared. At first I was weak as a little child, walking on legs I could not see.

"I slept during the morning, pulling a sheet over my eyes to shut out the light, and I was awakened again by a knocking. My strength had returned. I sat up and listened and heard talking. Soon the knocking was repeated and voices called. To gain time I answered them. My window opened on to a roof. I stepped through it, closed it, stood outside and watched. The old man and his two sons came into the room.

"You may imagine their surprise at finding the room empty. One of the younger men rushed to the window at once, flung it open and stared out. His eyes, and thick-lipped, bearded face came close to my face. He looked right through me. So did the others. The old man went and looked under the bed.

"While they were all talking together I came back into the room, slipped past them, and went down the stairs. In one room I found a box of matches, and when they had come down I returned to my room and set fire to the paper and straw, the bedding and the furniture."

"You set the house on fire?"

"Set the house on fire! Yes. It was the only way to cover my tracks.[1] I went out into the street."

So Kemp listened. It was the story of how the Invisible Man had got some clothes, how he lived by getting food and drink wherever he could, of the shelter he found and the beds he slept in, until he came to Iping.

---

[1] To stop people finding out what I had done.

CHAPTER 19

THE PLAN THAT FAILED

"But now," said Kemp, looking out of the window, "what are we to do?"

He moved nearer to his guest so that he should not see the three men who were coming up the hill road—too slowly, as it seemed to Kemp.

"What were you planning to do, when you came to Port Burdock? Had you any plan?"

"I was going to leave the country. But I have rather changed that plan since seeing you. I thought it would be wise, now the weather is hot, to make for the south. Especially as my secret was known, and everyone would be on the look-out for a muffled man. You have a line of steamers from here to France. My idea was to get on board one. Then I could go by train into Spain, or else to Algiers. It would not be difficult. There a man might be invisible always, and yet live. And do things. I was using that tramp as a money-box and carrier, until I decided how to get my books and things sent over to meet me."

"That's clear."

"And then he tried to rob me! He *has* hidden my books, Kemp. Hidden my books!—If I can get hold of him! . . ."

"Best plan to get the books from him first."

"But where is he? Do you know?"

"He's in the town police station, locked up, by his own request, in the strongest cell in the place."

"Cur!"[1] said the Invisible Man.

"But that hinders your plans a little."

"We must get those books; those books are necessary."

[1] Dog.

"Certainly," said Kemp, a little nervously, wondering if he heard footsteps outside. "Certainly we must get those books. But that won't be difficult, if he doesn't know they're for you."

"No," said the Invisible Man, thoughtfully.

Kemp tried to think of something to keep the talk going, but the Invisible Man went on of his own accord.

"Coming into your house, Kemp," he said, "changes all my plans. For you are a man that can understand. You are a scientist. You have told no one I am here?"

"Not a soul."

"If we are to make any use of being invisible, we must start by killing."

"Killing?" repeated Kemp. "I'm listening to your plan; but I'm not agreeing, mind. Why *killing*?"

"The point is: they know as well as we that there is an Invisible Man—and that Invisible Man, Kemp, must now start a Reign of Terror.[1] Yes; I mean it. A Reign of Terror. He must take some town, like your Burdock, and terrify it. He must give orders. He can do that in many ways. And everybody who disobeys his orders he must kill, and everybody who would defend them."

"Really!" said Kemp, no longer listening to Griffin, but to the sound of his front door opening and closing.

The Invisible Man had also heard the sound. "Hush!" he said. "What is that downstairs?"

"Nothing," said Kemp; and suddenly he began to speak loud and fast. "I don't agree to this, Griffin," he said. "Understand me, I don't agree to this. Why do you wish to be alone? Why not tell everyone? Think how much better it would be. You might have a million helpers."

The Invisible Man raised his hand. "There are footsteps coming upstairs," he said.

"Nonsense," said Kemp.

"Let me see," said the Invisible Man, and went to the door. And then things happened very swiftly. Kemp tried to stop

[1] A time when terrible things are done.

him. . . . Suddenly the clothes opened, sat down, the unseen man began to undress. Kemp opened the door.

As he opened, there came sounds of hurrying feet and voices downstairs.

With a quick movement Kemp pushed the Invisible Man back, jumped aside, and slammed the door. The key was outside and ready. In another moment Griffin would have been locked in the room—but for one little thing. The key fell noisily on the floor.

Kemp's face became white. He tried to grip the door-handle with both hands. For a moment he stood pulling. Then the door gave[1] six inches. But he got it closed again. The second time it was opened a foot, and the clothes came into the opening. Kemp's throat was gripped by invisible fingers, and he left his hold on the handle to defend himself. He was forced back and thrown heavily to the floor.

Half-way up the staircase was Colonel Adye, the chief of the Burdock police. He was staring at the sudden appearance of Kemp, followed by the clothes which danced in the air. He saw Kemp fall and then struggle to his feet. He saw Kemp rush forward, and go down again.

Then suddenly he was struck. By nothing! A great weight, it seemed, jumped upon him, and he was thrown down the staircase. An invisible foot trod on his back, ghostly steps passed downstairs, he heard the two police officers in the hall shout and run, and the sound of the front door of the house as it shut.

He rolled over and sat up staring. He saw Kemp coming down the staircase, his face white and bleeding.

"My God!" cried Kemp, "I couldn't stop him! He's gone!"

[1] Opened.

CHAPTER 20

THE HUNTING OF THE INVISIBLE MAN

KEMP took some time to explain to Colonel Adye what had happened.

"He is mad," said Kemp; "a mad beast. Pure selfishness. He thinks of nothing but his own advantage, his own safety. I have listened this morning to a dreadful story of brutal self-seeking. . . . He has wounded men. He will kill them unless we can prevent him. He will create a terror. Nothing can stop him. He is going out now—mad!"

"He must be caught," said Adye. "That is certain."

"But how?" cried Kemp, and suddenly became full of ideas. "You must begin at once; you must set every man to work; you must prevent his leaving this place. Once he gets away he may go through the country as he wills, killing. The only thing that may keep him here is the thought of finding some books which he values very much. I will tell you about them. There is a man in your police station—Marvel."

"I know," said Adye, "I know. Those books—yes. But the Invisible Man. . . ."

"Says he hasn't got them. But he thinks Marvel has. Now, listen! You must prevent him from eating or sleeping—day and night the country must be on the watch for him. Food must be locked up, all food, so that he will have to break into a house or shop to get it. The houses everywhere must be shut against him; for twenty miles round Port Burdock the whole country must begin hunting and keep on hunting. I tell you, Adye, he is dangerous. Unless he is caught, it is frightful to think of the things that may happen."

"Come along," said Colonel Adye, "tell me as we go. What else is there we can do?"

In another moment Adye was leading the way downstairs. They found the front door open and the policeman standing outside staring at empty air. "He's got away, sir," said one.

"We must go to the police station at once," said Adye. "One of you go on down and report and then come up and meet us—quickly. And now, Kemp, what else?"

"Dogs," said Kemp. "Get dogs. They don't see him, but they smell him. Get dogs."

"Good," said Adye. "It's not generally known, but the prison officers over at Halstead know a man with bloodhounds. Dogs. What else?"

"Bear in mind," said Kemp, "his food shows. You can see it for some time after he has eaten it, so that he has to hide. You must keep on searching. Every quiet corner. And put away all weapons—and everything that might be a weapon. He can't carry such things for long. And you must hide anything he can pick up and strike men with."

"Good again," said Adye. "We'll have him yet!"

"And on the roads——" said Kemp, and hesitated.

"Yes?" said Adye.

"Broken glass," said Kemp. "It's cruel, I know. But think of what he may do!"

Adye drew the air in between his teeth sharply.

"It's cruel. I don't perhaps think we should. But I'll have some broken glass got ready. If he is killed, it will be only what he deserves. . . ."

"The man is mad, I tell you," said Kemp. "He will do anything. Our only chance is to be first. He has cut himself off from mankind."

CHAPTER 21

THE WICKSTEED MURDER

THE Invisible Man seems to have rushed out of Kemp's house in blind anger. A little child playing near Kemp's gateway was violently caught up and thrown aside—so that his leg was broken—and then for some hours he passed out of knowledge. No one knows where he went or what he did. But we can think of him hurrying through the hot June morning, up the hill and on to the open hill behind Port Burdock, and hiding at last in the woods.

There he hid for two hours, and a growing crowd of men were hunting him across the country with dogs, and searching for him in every direction. In the morning he had still been simply a story, a terror; in the afternoon, chiefly because of Kemp's dryly worded[1] notice, he was shown to be a real enemy, to be wounded, captured, or overcome, and the country-side began organizing itself very quickly. Even by two o'clock, he might still have escaped from the district, by getting on board a train, but after two that became impossible: every passenger train along the lines on a great piece of country between Southampton, Winchester, Brighton and Horsham travelled with locked doors, and the goods trains were almost entirely stopped. And in a great circle of twenty miles round Port Burdock men armed with guns and sticks were presently setting out in groups of three and four, with dogs, to search the roads and fields.

Mounted police rode along the country roads, stopping at every house and warning the people to lock up their houses and not go out unless they were armed. All the schools had

[1] Dryly worded = without any words which are not needed.

broken up[1] by three o'clock, and the frightened children, keeping together in groups, were hurrying home. Kemp's notice was put up everywhere, telling clearly what must be done—that the Invisible Man must have neither food nor sleep, that continual watch must be kept for signs of him. Before night the whole country was on guard. Before night came news, from mouth to mouth—the story of the murder of Mr. Wicksteed.

Somewhere on the road the Invisible Man must have picked up an iron bar. Mr. Wicksteed, a quiet and harmless man on his way home from work, had, no doubt, seen an iron bar walking by itself, and had turned to follow it. Perhaps the Invisible Man mistook him for one of the hunters. At any rate he stopped this quiet little Mr. Wicksteed, attacked him, broke his arm, knocked him down and beat his head to pieces.

Then there is the story of a Voice heard by some men in a field, laughing and crying. Across the field it went and was lost. The Invisible Man must have seen the use Kemp had made of his story. He must have found all the houses shut and locked, and seen the groups of men with dogs watching. He knew that he was a hunted man. In the night he must have eaten and slept, for on the last morning he was himself again and ready for his struggle against the world.

[1] Closed for some time.

CHAPTER 22

THE SIEGE OF KEMP'S HOUSE

KEMP was reading a strange letter, written in pencil on a dirty sheet of paper.

"You have been very clever," this letter ran, "though what you gain by it I cannot think. You are against me. For a whole day you have hunted me—you have tried to rob me of a night's rest. But I have had food in spite of you, I have slept in spite of you, and we are only beginning. We are only beginning. There is nothing to be done but to start the Terror. This is the first day of the Terror. Port Burdock is no longer under the Queen, tell your police, and the rest of them; it is under me —the Terror! I am Invisible Man the First. We shall begin with the death of a man named Kemp. He will die to-day. He may hide himself away, and get guards around him; Death, the unseen Death, is coming. The game begins. Death starts. Help him not, my people, lest Death fall upon you also. To-day Kemp is to die."

Kemp read this letter twice. "That's his voice!" he said, "and he means it."

He got up slowly, leaving his lunch unfinished—the letter had come by the one o'clock post—and went into his study. He rang the bell for his servant, and told her to go round the house at once, see that all the windows were shut, and close all the shutters. He closed the shutters of his study himself. From a locked drawer in his bedroom he took a little revolver, examined it carefully, and put it into his pocket. He wrote a number of short notes, one to Colonel Adye, and gave them to his servant to take.

"There is no danger to you," he said. He thought for a time and then returned to his meal.

81

Finally he struck the table. "We will have him!" he said. "He will come too far."

He went up to his room, carefully shutting every door after him. "It's a game," he said, "a strange game—but I shall win, Mr. Griffin," he said.

He stood at the window staring at the hot hill-side. "He must get food every day. Did he really sleep last night? Out in the open somewhere? I wish we could get some good cold, wet weather instead of the heat. He may be watching me now."

He went close to the window. Something hit the wall above the window.

"I'm getting nervous," said Kemp. But it was five minutes before he went to the window again. "It must have been a bird," he said.

Soon he heard the front-door bell ringing and hurried downstairs. He unbolted and unlocked the door, and opened without showing himself. It was Adye. "Your servant's been attacked, Kemp," he said round the door.

"What!" exclaimed Kemp.

"She had that note of yours taken away from her. He's very near. Let me in."

Kemp opened the door a few inches, and Adye came in. He stood in the hall, looking at Kemp fastening the door.

Kemp swore.

"What a fool I was!" said Kemp. "I might have known. . . . Already!"

"What is the matter?" said Adye.

"Look here!" said Kemp, and led the way into his study. He handed Adye the Invisible Man's letter.

Adye read it. "And you——?" said Adye.

The sound of a breaking window came from upstairs. Adye saw the little revolver half out of Kemp's pocket. "It's a window upstairs!" said Kemp, and led the way up. There came a second noise while they were still on the staircase. When they reached the study they found two of the three windows broken, half the room full of broken glass, and one big stone lying on the writing-table. The two men stopped in the doorway. Kemp swore again, and as he did so the third window broke with a crack like a pistol, and the broken glass fell into the room.

"What's this for?" said Adye.

"It is beginning," said Kemp.

"There is no way of climbing up here?"

"Not even for a cat," said Kemp.

Stones came flying in and then it sounded as if someone was hammering at the shuttered windows downstairs. The two men stood on the landing not knowing what to do.

"I know!" said Adye. "Let me have a stick or something, and I'll go down to the station and get the man with the bloodhounds. They'll find him."

Another window broke.

"You haven't a revolver?" asked Adye.

Kemp's hand went to his pocket. Then he hesitated. "I haven't one—at least to spare."

"I'll bring it back," said Adye. "You'll be safe here."

Kemp gave him the weapon.

"Now for the door," said Adye.

As they stood waiting in the hall, they heard one of the bedroom windows crack. Kemp went to the door and began to slip back the bolts as silently as he could. His face was a little paler than usual.

"You must step straight out," said Kemp.

In another moment Adye was on the doorstep and the door was shut. He waited for a moment, feeling more comfortable with his back against the door. Then he marched down the steps. He crossed the grass and approached the gate. Something moved near him.

"Stop a bit," said a Voice, and Adye stopped, with his hand on the revolver.

"Well?" said Adye.

"Please go back to the house," said the Voice.

"No," said Adye. He thought of trying a shot in the direction of the Voice.

"What are you going to do?" said the Voice.

"What I do is my own business," said Adye.

The words were still on his lips, when an arm came round his neck, he felt a knee in his back, and his head was forced backward. He drew and fired wildly, and in another moment he was struck in the mouth and the revolver was taken from his hand. He tried to struggle up and fell back. "Damn!" said Adye. The Voice laughed.

"I would kill you now if it wasn't the waste of a bullet," it said. He saw the revolver in the air, six feet off, pointed at him.

"Well?" said Adye, sitting up.

"Get up," said the Voice.

Adye stood up.

"Stand still," said the Voice, and then firmly, "Don't try any tricks. Remember I can see your face, if you can't see mine. You've got to go back to the house."

"He won't let me in," said Adye.

"That's a pity," said the Invisible Man. "It isn't you I want to kill."

Adye glanced away from the revolver, and saw the sea far off, very blue and dark under the bright sun, the smooth green hill, the white rocks of the coast, and the spreading town, and suddenly he knew that life was very sweet. His eyes came back to this little metal thing hanging between heaven and earth, six feet away. "What am I to do?" he said.

"What am *I* to do?" asked the Invisible Man. "If I let you go, you will get help. The only thing is for you to go back to the house."

"I'll try. If he lets me in, will you promise not to rush the door?"

"I don't want to fight *you*," said the Voice.

Kemp had hurried upstairs after letting Adye out, and now, looking through a broken window, he saw Adye stand talking with the unseen. "Why doesn't he fire?" said Kemp to himself. Then the revolver moved a little.

"That's strange!" he said. "Adye has given up the revolver."

"Promise not to rush the door," Adye was saying. "Give me a chance."

"You go back to the house. I tell you I'll promise nothing."

Adye seemed to decide suddenly. He turned towards the house, and walked slowly with his hands behind him. Kemp watched him. The revolver appeared, a little dark thing, following Adye. Then things happened very quickly. Adye jumped at the little thing, missed it, threw up his hands and fell forward on his face. A little ball of blue smoke rose into the air. Kemp did not hear the sound of the shot. Adye raised himself on one arm, fell forward, and lay still.

For a time Kemp remained looking at Adye as he lay peacefully on the grass. The day was very hot and still, nothing seemed to move. Adye lay on the lawn near the gate. The curtains of all the houses down the hill road were drawn, but in one little green summer-house was a white figure, apparently an old man asleep. Kemp's eyes came back to Adye—the game was not beginning well!

Then came a ringing and a knocking at the front door, but the servants had locked themselves into their rooms. Silence followed. Kemp sat listening and then began to look carefully out of the three windows, one after another. He went to the stairs and stood listening anxiously. He wondered what his enemy was doing.

Suddenly there was a hammering from below. He waited and went down the stairs again. The house was loud with the sound of heavy blows and breaking wood. He went into the kitchen. The door was being broken down by an axe.

Kemp went back into the passage, trying to think. In a moment the Invisible Man would be in the kitchen. This door would not keep him a moment, and then——

The front-door bell rang again. It would be the policemen with the maid. He ran into the hall, opened the door, and three people fell into the house in a heap, and Kemp shut the door again.

"The Invisible Man!" said Kemp. "He has a revolver—

with two shots left. He's killed Adye. Shot him at least. Didn't you see him on the grass? He's lying there."

"Who?" said one of the policemen.

"Adye," said Kemp.

"We came round the back way," said the girl.

"What's that hammering?" asked one of the policemen.

"He's in the kitchen—or will be. He has found an axe——"

Suddenly the house was full of the sound of the Invisible Man's blows on the kitchen door. The girl stared towards the kitchen and stepped into the dining-room. Kemp tried to explain in broken sentences. They heard the kitchen door breaking open.

"This way," cried Kemp, starting quickly, and he pushed the policemen into the dining-room doorway.

"Poker," said Kemp, and rushed to the fire.

He handed a poker to each of the policemen.

He suddenly threw himself backwards. "Whup," said one policeman, jumped aside, and caught the axe on his poker. The revolver cracked and shot a hole in a picture. The second policeman brought his poker down on the little weapon and sent it to the floor.

The axe went back into the passage. They could hear the Invisible Man breathing. "Stand away, you two," he said. "I want that man Kemp."

"We want you," said the first policeman, making a quick step forward and striking with his poker at the Voice. The Invisible Man must have started back, and blundered into a chair.

Then, as the policeman went after him, the Invisible Man returned and struck him down.

But the second policeman, aiming behind the axe with his poker, hit something soft that snapped. There was a sharp cry of pain, and then the axe fell to the ground. The policeman struck again at emptiness and hit nothing; he put his foot on the axe and struck again. Then he stood, holding the poker, listening for the slightest movement.

He heard the window open, and a quick rush of feet within.

His companion rolled over and sat up, with the blood running down between his eye and ear. "Where is he?" asked the man on the floor.

"Don't know. I've hit him. He's standing somewhere in the hall unless he's slipped past you. Dr. Kemp—sir!"

"Dr. Kemp," cried the policeman again.

The second policeman began struggling to his feet. He stood up. Suddenly the faint sound of bare feet could be heard. "Whup!" cried the first policeman, and threw his poker.

He started to go after the Invisible Man. Then he changed his mind and stepped into the dining-room.

"Dr. Kemp——" he began, and stopped short.

The dining-room window was wide open, and neither maid nor Kemp was to be seen.

CHAPTER 23

THE HUNTER HUNTED

KEMP had set off running, running for life as he had seen Mr. Marvel run down the hill road. Never, he thought, had he seemed to run so slowly.

People looked at him. They saw fear in his face.

. . . He was rushing to the town below where people were standing or moving in groups.

He slowed down and then heard swift footsteps behind. "The Invisible Man," he cried. He thought of going into the police station, but changed his mind, turned down a side street and then into a yard, into a little house and so back into the main road.

A crowd had gathered, there was a noise of running feet. A big man, a few yards away, was swinging a heavy spade, striking at something. Another man came out of a shop with a thick stick in his hand. "Spread out! Spread out!" cried someone. Kemp stopped and looked round, breathing heavily. "He's close here!" he cried. "Form a line across——"

He was hit hard under the ear, and trying to face round towards his unseen enemy, he struck in the air. Then he was hit again under the jaw, and fell to the ground. In another moment a knee was digging into his chest, hands gripped his throat, but one hand was weaker than the other; then the spade of the big man came through the air above him, and struck something. He felt blood warm on his face. The hold on his throat was loosened and Kemp rolled on top. "I've got him!" cried Kemp. "Help! help—hold him! He's down! Hold his feet!"

In another second there was a rush of people to the struggle.

There was no shouting after Kemp's cry—only a sound of blows and feet and heavy breathing.

Then the Invisible Man got to his feet. Kemp clung to his legs. Then someone got hold of his neck and pulled him back. Down went the heap of struggling, kicking men again. Then suddenly came a wild cry that died away into silence.

"Get back!" cried Kemp. "He's hurt, I tell you. Stand back."

A doctor was feeling the unseen body.

"The mouth is all wet," he said.

He stood up quickly, and then kneeled down on the ground by the side of the thing unseen. Fresh people came to increase the pushing crowd. Men were coming out of the houses. The doors of the inn stood suddenly wide open. Very little was said. Kemp felt around him; his hands seemed to pass through empty air. "He's not breathing," he said, and then, "I cannot feel his heart. His side—ugh!"

An old woman, looking under the arm of the big man with the spade, screamed sharply. "Look there!" she said, and pointed. And looking where she pointed, everyone saw a shadowy, cloudy body. At first, they could see through it, but it became more solid every moment.

"Hallo!" cried the policeman. "Here's his feet showing!"

And so, slowly, beginning at his hands and feet, and going slowly along his limbs to the centre of his body, that strange change continued. It was like the slow spreading of a poison. First came the white form of a limb, then the glassy bones, then the flesh and skin, first a faint mist which became thicker and harder and more solid. Presently they could see his chest and his shoulders, and the dim shape of his face.

When at last the crowd made way for Kemp to stand erect, there lay, naked and pitiful on the ground, the broken body of a young man about thirty. His hair was white—not grey with age, but white as snow—and his eyes were bright like jewels. His expression was one of anger and fear.

"Cover his face!" cried a man. "For God's sake cover that face!"

Someone brought a sheet. They covered him, and carried him into the inn. And there it was, on a bed in an ill-lighted bedroom, among a crowd of excited people, that Griffin, the first of all men to make himself invisible, ended his strange and terrible life.

QUESTIONS

CHAPTER 1

1. In what month did the stranger come?
2. What did Mrs. Hall tell Millie to do?
3. How did the stranger hide his face?
4. Where did the stranger put his hat and coat?
5. Why did Mrs. Hall take away his clothes?
6. His mouth must have been damaged in an accident. Who thought this, and why?
7. Where were the stranger's boxes?
8. What happened to Tom, and why was he " tied up "?

CHAPTER 2

1. What did the clock-mender say when he came into the bar?
2. Was the lamp lighted in the dark room? If not, how was Mrs. Hall able to see the stranger?
3. How did the stranger stare at Mr. Henfrey?
4. How did the stranger explain why he had to sit in a dark room?
5. Why did Henfrey take so long in mending the clock?
6. There was only one thing wrong with the clock. What was it?
7. What did Mrs. Hall dream about?

CHAPTER 3

1. How many (a) trunks; (b) boxes of books; (c) boxes and cases full of glass bottles arrived at Iping?
2. What did the dog do to the stranger? (Five actions.)
3. What happened to Hall when he opened the bedroom door?
4. What did the lady want to do to the dog?
5. Mention as many kinds of bottles as you can that were in the boxes. How many cases were emptied?
6. When the stranger went to work he did not trouble in the least about—what? (Four things.)
7. " Put down a shilling in my bill." What does this mean? And why should Mrs. Hall put it down?
8. What did Fearenside think was the reason for the stranger's hiding his face?

CHAPTER 4

1. What did Mrs. Hall mean when she said the stranger " discovered things "?

91

2. What did the young men do when the stranger passed them in the village street? (Three things.)
3. Describe the appearance of Cuss when he came out of the stranger's room.
4. "Give me something to drink." Who said this, and why?
5. What pulled the doctor's nose? And why did Bunting laugh?

CHAPTER 5

1. What did Mrs. Bunting hear when she listened?
2. What did Mr. Bunting hear?
3. If you had been Mr. Bunting, would you have done what Mr. Bunting did? If so, why? If not, why not?
4. What could Mr. Bunting see through the half-open door? (Three things.)
5. What is "housekeeping money"?
6. Why did the thief sneeze?
7. Why was the light of the candle unnecessary?

CHAPTER 6

1. What did Hall expect to see when he opened the bedroom door? Why did he expect to see what he did?
2. What happened when Mrs. Hall put her hand on the pillow? (Three things.)
3. "To think it should rise against me now. . . ." What is it that makes the furniture "rise against" Mrs. Hall?
4. What did Mr. Wadgers say when they waked him? And what did he mean?
5. What did he want first? Why did they not first break down the door?
6. "And that was all." What was all?

CHAPTER 7

1. How many hours did the stranger remain in the parlour? How do you know?
2. What happened when he rang the bell? Why did no one answer it?
3. Why did Mrs. Hall bring the unpaid bill?
4. "I wonder where you found it?" Where does Mrs. Hall think the stranger got the money? Does she really wonder? Why not?
5. What does Mrs. Hall want to know? (Three things.)
6. When the people saw *nothing*, what did they expect to see?
7. How many people collected round the inn door? What made them collect there?
8. How did the stranger deal with Jaffers, Hall and Wadgers?
9. What did the figure have in each hand?

10. "It seemed to meet something in the air." What did Huxter's hand meet?
11. Why was Jaffers ordered to take the stranger in charge?
12. Why was the stranger able to escape from so many people?

CHAPTER 8

1. Why did the tramp hate his boots?
2. Why did he think he had gone mad?
3. "He turned round and saw . . ." What did he see?
4. Although the stranger was invisible, he still needed things. What did he need?
5. "And then comes . . . out of heaven." What came out of the empty sky?
6. "Mr. Marvel was . . ." Describe Mr. Marvel in three short sentences.
7. Why was he wiping his mouth when he came out of the inn?

CHAPTER 9

1. What were Mr. Cuss and Mr. Bunting doing?
2. Why was Mr. Bunting unable to lift his head?
3. What had the Invisible Man come to collect?—and why?

CHAPTER 10

1. What strange noises came from the parlour? Who were making them?
2. What was Mrs. Hall looking at, and why did she not see what she was looking at?
3. Why did Huxter shout "Stop thief!"? Was there any thief? And could they stop him?
4. What happened to Huxter, Hall and two workmen who tried to "stop the thief"?
5. Why was Mr. Cuss wearing a tablecloth?
6. Describe Mr. Cuss's first few minutes after running out of the inn.
7. How was Mr. Bunting trying to clothe himself? Why?

CHAPTER 11

1. Where was Mr. Marvel walking? How did he look? What was he carrying?
2. Was it night or day? How do you know?
3. What did the Invisible Man order the tramp to do?

CHAPTER 12

1. Whose clothes had Mr. Marvel left in the woods? Why had he left them there?

2. Why did he look about him with terror?
3. How much of the story did the sailor tell Mr. Marvel?
4. " He rose stiffly from his seat, as if in pain." What had happened to Mr. Marvel?
5. Why did he say that the story in the paper was a lie?
6. How did a fist full of money travel " of its own accord "?
7. What made money " quietly walk away " from the bank, shops and inns?

CHAPTER 13

1. How many windows had Mr. Kemp's study? In what directions did they look? What was there in the room?
2. What did the doctor see from his window?
3. At what time of day was it? How do you know?
4. What did people do when they heard the rushing sound? (Five things.)

CHAPTER 14

1. " He spoke like . . . ate . . . and talked . . ." Fill in these spaces. Can you describe the speaker?
2. Why did the black-bearded man keep one hand behind him?
3. " If he comes . . ." said the black-bearded man. Finish his sentence, by saying what he wished his hearers to understand.
4. " I know what country I'm in." What does he mean by these words?
5. Did the pistol-bullet hit the Invisible Man? How do you know?
6. " The voice of the Invisible Man was heard for the first time." Why was he silent at first, and why did he cry out?
7. Why did the bearded man move his hand a little when he was shooting?

CHAPTER 15

1. For how long did Dr. Kemp stand looking out of the window? How long afterwards did the door bell ring?
2. " No one there." Who was really at the door?
3. What was the dark spot on the floor? What was there on the door handle?
4. What did the doctor see between himself and the bed? Why did he not grasp the thing?
5. What did the Invisible Man do to Kemp? (Three things.)
6. " The maddest thing I've ever seen in my life." What had Kemp seen?
7. What did Kemp bring from the kitchen?
8. Why did the Invisible Man not need a knife?
9. " They all get frightened at me." Who were some of the people who got frightened, and why did they?

CHAPTER 16

1. How did the Invisible Man make sure that he was safe in Kemp's bedroom?
2. What sound did Kemp hear? Why did the Invisible Man make that sound?
3. "I meant to keep it a secret." Why could he not keep it a secret?

CHAPTER 17

1. Why should the Invisible Man curse because his story was in the papers?
2. "It was a long explanation." What was he trying to explain?
3. What will happen if you drop a little oil on white paper?
4. What did Kemp nearly forget?
5. Why could the Invisible Man do nothing?
6. Why did his father shoot himself?

CHAPTER 18

1. Where did the Invisible Man take a room? What kind of a room was it?
2. Why is he so anxious to get his books back?
3. What happened when he tried white wool?
4. How long did it take to make the cat invisible? What upset her, and why?
5. Why did the landlord want to know what had happened?
6. Why did the Invisible Man think it was time to disappear?
7. What did his hands look like before they disappeared?
8. Where did the Invisible Man go when his landlord came into the room? Where did the landlord look for him?
9. Why did the Invisible Man set fire to the house?

CHAPTER 19

1. What was the Invisible Man planning to do at first?
2. How was he using the tramp?
3. Where was the tramp? Why had he asked to go there?
4. What will the Invisible Man start?
5. What will he do to those who disobey him?
6. "Then things happened very swiftly." Describe four things that happened.
7. Who was on the staircase? What happened to him?
8. What did the police officers do?

CHAPTER 20

1. " He thinks of nothing but . . . I have listened to . . . He will create . . ." Fill in these spaces, and then say what it all makes Kemp think of the Invisible Man.
2. What is the only thing that will keep the Invisible Man here?
3. What other things should be done? With weapons? On the roads?
4. " It will be only what he deserves." What does the Invisible Man deserve, and why?

CHAPTER 21

1. What happened to the little child?
2. For how long did the Invisible Man hide, and where?
3. He was " a real enemy ". What should be done with him?
4. What did the mounted police do? (Three things.)
5. What did Kemp's notice say should be done?
6. What had Mr. Wicksteed seen, and what did he do when he saw it?
7. What was the Voice doing?

CHAPTER 22

1. What orders did Kemp give to his servant?
2. What did he take from a locked drawer, and what did he do with it?
3. Why did he tell his servant that there was no danger to her?
4. " It must have been a bird." Was it a bird? If not, what was it?
5. What did they find in the study? (Three things.)
6. How did Adye think he could help to catch the Invisible Man?
7. First Adye wanted a stick, then he wanted a revolver. Why did he change his mind?
8. Why did he feel more comfortable with his back to the door?
9. What did Adye see when he looked away from the revolver? (Four things.)
10. Why did nobody go to the door when the bell rang?
11. Who were the three people who fell into the house in a heap?

CHAPTER 23

1. What weapons did people use to kill the Invisible Man?
2. In how many places was Kemp hit by the Invisible Man? What were they?
3. What did people see first? What happened to it?
4. What lay on the ground at the end?